AF580786

BIG SKY RANCHER

JoAnna Sims

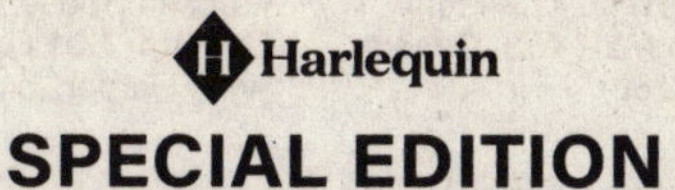
Harlequin
SPECIAL EDITION

If you purchased this book without a cover you should be aware that this book is stolen property. It was reported as "unsold and destroyed" to the publisher, and neither the author nor the publisher has received any payment for this "stripped book."

Recycling programs for this product may not exist in your area.

ISBN-13: 978-1-335-18045-2

Big Sky Rancher

Copyright © 2026 by JoAnna Sims

All rights reserved. No part of this book may be used or reproduced in any manner whatsoever without written permission.

Without limiting the exclusive rights of any author, contributor or the publisher of this publication, any unauthorized use of this publication to train generative artificial intelligence (AI) technologies is expressly prohibited. Harlequin also exercises their rights under Article 4(3) of the Digital Single Market Directive 2019/790 and expressly reserves this publication from the text and data mining exception.

This is a work of fiction. Names, characters, places and incidents are either the product of the author's imagination or are used fictitiously. Any resemblance to actual persons, living or dead, businesses, companies, events or locales is entirely coincidental.

For questions and comments about the quality of this book, please contact us at CustomerService@Harlequin.com.

TM and ® are trademarks of Harlequin Enterprises ULC.

Harlequin Enterprises ULC
22 Adelaide St. West, 41st Floor
Toronto, Ontario M5H 4E3, Canada
www.Harlequin.com

HarperCollins Publishers
Macken House, 39/40 Mayor Street Upper,
Dublin 1, D01 C9W8, Ireland
www.HarperCollins.com

Printed in Lithuania

1 2 3 4 5 6 7 8 9 10 LIT 28 27 26 25

Rowan looked at him. "Are you staying or going?"

I should say that I'm going. Early morning, long day of ranching ahead. "Staying."

That earned him the smallest of smiles, and it only made him hungry for more. As he followed Spitfire to the dance floor, Axel began to feel something inside that he hadn't felt in too many years to count. That initial attraction had unexpectedly grown into interest and curiosity.

When the band bid everyone a good night, Rowan held out her hand to him and said, "Thank you for the dancing."

"My pleasure."

They said good-night and he watched her walk in the opposite direction. And realized that he didn't know Rowan's last name or if she lived in Bozeman or was just visiting. He'd wanted to ask for her number, but he'd been around long enough to know better. And in his defense, he'd been distracted by her eyes.

"Amateur," Axel scolded himself, looking up at the sliver of moon above. "You let that one get away."

Dear Reader,

Thank you for choosing *Big Sky Rancher*, a Brands of Montana romance.

Twenty-five-year-old Rowan Brand is having a rough time, to put it mildly. She is a small-town Wyoming cowgirl who has it all. She was a local celebrity, engaged to the love of her life, Dutton Grange, and she had a flourishing YouTube channel focused on everything happily-ever-after, which she had launched to document her own magical journey to "I do!" Life was positively exciting and wonderful and perfect, until her fiancé dumped her at their rehearsal dinner in front of all of their friends, family and her followers live streaming.

Humiliated and horrified, Rowan retreated to Hideaway Ranch in Big Sky, Montana, to lick her wounds and to figure out next steps. What she wasn't prepared for was to have her head turned so quickly when she met a sexy rancher by the name of Axel Redford. He was smooth-talking and offering her a great time, so Rowan figured: Why not date the no-strings-attached cowboy? She was single, wasn't she? Unexpectedly, Rowan began to catch some feelings for Axel. And that made her wonder: Was Axel a rebound or was he that happily-ever-after she had always dreamed about?

I hope you love Axel and Rowan's story as much as I enjoyed writing it!

Happy reading!

JoAnna

Website: JoannaSimsRomance.Love

JoAnna Sims is proud to pen contemporary romance for Harlequin Special Edition. JoAnna's series, The Brands of Montana, features hardworking characters with hometown values. You are cordially invited to join the Brands of Montana as they wrangle their own happily-ever-afters.

Books by JoAnna Sims

Harlequin Special Edition

The Brands of Montana

Big Sky Rancher
A Match Made in Montana
High Country Christmas
High Country Baby
Meet Me at the Chapel
Thankful for You
A Wedding to Remember
A Bride for Liam Brand
High Country Cowgirl
The Sergeant's Christmas Mission
Her Second Forever
His Christmas Eve Homecoming
She Dreamed of a Cowboy
The Marine's Christmas Wish
Her Outback Rancher
Big Sky Cowboy
Big Sky Christmas

Visit the Author Profile page at Harlequin.com for more titles.

This book is dedicated to:

Victoria H., Editorial Services

&

Jenn O., Content Management

Thank you for working every day
to make our books as perfect as they can be.

Prologue

Twenty-five-year-old Rowan Brand was flying high. In a very short amount of time, hers would be the biggest wedding Laramie, Wyoming, had ever seen. She would be marrying Dutton Grange, the love of her life and the soon-to-be father of her at least three children. Rowan had imagined the day she would get married. She kept a wedding binder overflowing with dress ideas, cake ideas and DIY hacks. All she needed was a perfect husband—Dutton Grange—and she had always known she was destined to be Dutton's wife.

Today she was picking out the dress she would be wearing during their rehearsal and dinner tonight. The wedding was three weeks away, but they had moved up the rehearsal to allow Dutton's baby brother, Decon, to share in some of the festivities before he headed off to the Navy's Recruit Training and Command at Great Lakes, Illinois. She didn't mind moving it up. She loved her soon-to-be brother-in-law. The only thing that did bother her was what to wear for the evening. It wasn't like her to procrastinate, especially when it came to the wedding. But for whatever unfathomable reason, she had saved this dress to the last minute. And because she was always faithful with wedding updates on her socials—posting on her How True Love Found Me YouTube channel and getting follower input on just about anything wedding related—it felt odd to have her socials dark during this dress fitting. Her followers had begun to feel like a part of her extended family.

She examined her reflection in the mirror; in her younger years, she had been on the chunky side, and her fair skin, face full of freckles and thick, copper red hair had made her the butt of many jokes and a target for bullies. But while her friend Mercy Adams would comfort her and tell her how pretty she was, her other dear friend Cassady "Cassius Clay" Abbott would punch them in the nose or put her boot on the bully's hind parts and push them face-first to the ground. Once everyone knew that Cassady was her protector, they left her alone. Rowan always felt blessed that a simple alphabetic seating arrangement in kindergarten had turned the three of them into the best of friends.

And now that she was grown, her hair had turned a lovely auburn with copper highlights, still thick and wavy. She wore it long to the small of her back. Her freckles had softened, and now, in her opinion, they gave her a youthful look. She was five-seven in her bare feet and still had some curves. But she had done the internal work to embrace herself and her body. Yet, the scars of the bullying were still with her, no matter how hard she tried to rid herself of them.

"What do you think?" Rowan asked Cassady and Mercy.

"You look just like Ariel from *Little Mermaid*."

Mercy welled up, the emotional one of the bunch. She snapped off a few shots to show her.

"Without the shell pasties and the inability to walk on land as a possible barrier to the longevity of the marriage," Cassady said, the official sarcastic one of the trio. She was lounging on her back on her purple crushed-velvet settee, eyes mainly on her phone. "But on the other hand, Dutton may be a freak in bed. You don't know. Don't take it off your roster entirely. You on the bed, with pasties and a tail? White-hot honeymoon."

"Why do you always have to be so terrible?" Mercy frowned at Cassady. "Don't listen to her, Rowan. You look beautiful."

Cassady shrugged. "You say I'm terrible, I say I am being an excellent friend giving an honest response."

Rowan examined the photos and then at her image again in the full-length mirror. Perhaps this was too shiny and cupcake-ish for her rehearsal dinner.

"Would you unzip me?" she asked Mercy. "I'm definitely not going for a Disney princess look. But," she added, "I'd wear just about anything to get Dutton in the mood to make a baby on our honeymoon."

Cassady scoffed. "Is he really going to do the deed? He's been keeping you on ice for over a year."

"It will be our wedding night," Rowan reminded her doubting friend.

Rowan slipped the next dress on, and Mercy zipped it up. It was a sedate navy wrap that had dainty pearl details down the back. It was demure with a 1950s housewife vibe. The Granges, like just about everyone else in Wyoming, were God-fearing and conservative. They would *love* this dress.

"I like this one," Mercy said as she quickly plaited Rowan's hair into a French braid before she took photos at all angles for her to see.

It wasn't her style. The blue was too dark, the cut of the fabric boxy and stuffy, and the pearls were too old-fashioned. After looking at the photos, she couldn't seem to bring herself to like it, but she wanted to please her soon-to-be in-laws. So what if she wore a dress that would meet their approval for just one night?

"What do you think, Cass?" Rowan turned her back to the mirror.

Cassady looked up from her phone. "If you like it, then that's good enough for me."

"Why are you holding back?" Rowan asked, feeling a smidge irritated. "Tell the truth."

Mercy wore a worried expression on her lovely round face. She was a worrier and when their trio wasn't in perfect harmony, she became anxious. "Honesty isn't always the best policy," she interjected, clasping her hands together.

Cassady sat up and put her phone down. "That dress doesn't suit you. We all know that, and I'm tired of pretending that this wedding is a good idea."

"Why do you have to be so mean, Cassady?" Mercy asked with a shake of the head.

"Why don't you like Dutton?" Rowan asked, hands on her waist.

"He's a pathetic weak little boy for a start." Cassady stood up. "Dutton got his poor fragile heart broken and then decided to reset his virginity! So, he decided to follow his parents' teaching and save himself for marriage."

"That doesn't make him weak." Rowan frowned. "It's not easy to save yourself for marriage."

"Admirable." Mercy nodded.

"Give me a break," Cassady snapped back. "He's not a virgin! He doesn't just get to reset it. He could say I'm waiting this time for marriage, but he doesn't get to parade around acting like he's as pure as the driven snow."

Mercy moved to stand next to Rowan for support.

"I wish you would try to like him," Rowan said. Cassady was her bestie for life, and Dutton would be her one true love until the end of her life. Eventually they would have to accept each other. Wouldn't they?

Cassady's expression softened. "I love you. And because I love you, I will try."

"And don't hit him again," Mercy interjected.

"Hey!" Cassady said with a sheepish half smile and a twinkle in her dark brown eyes. "That was middle school. And he deserved it."

Later that day, dressed in her navy dress, with her grandmother's matching pearl earrings and choker, she had finished the look with a pair of navy kitten heels to make sure she wasn't taller than Dutton. He was rather short and stocky, and she loved that about him. And although she loved her high heels, they were easy to give up so her future husband could feel more confident standing beside her.

"Oh, Rowan." Her mother, Marla, embraced her

when she arrived at the church for the rehearsal. "You look so beautiful. I can't believe that my baby is finally getting married. Praise the Lord, I can see those grandbaby blessings that are coming into my life. We both know your brother isn't going to be any help in that department."

"Oh, Mama. I hope so," she said, ignoring the comment about her older brother by two years, Denver. Today was about her.

Not too soon after, the guests were flowing into the church: her cousins, her friends from school, and all of Dutton's large, extended family. And, of course, Denver bringing up the rear, his hair still wet from a shower, his shirt barely buttoned.

"Did you invite the entire town?" Cassady had arrived, wearing men's pleated black pants, a bold patterned button-down shirt and sneakers with the same print as the shirt.

"Nearly," Rowan said. "I just couldn't say no to anyone."

It wasn't common to invite all the wedding guests to the rehearsal dinner, but she had an uncommon love with Dutton, not to mention the fact that this would make incredible content for her channel. She had hired a talented videographer whose online videos were amazing and went viral every single time. She flew him in for the rehearsal, and she had a round-trip ticket for him to shoot the wedding.

"Here," Cassady said. "Let me demonstrate how to say it. No-wah!"

Rowan decided to redirect the conversation. "Are you set for Montana?"

"Roger that."

Rowan had discovered that she had distant triplet Brand cousins, Charlotte, Rayna and Danica, who owned Hideaway Ranch in Big Sky, Montana. The destination ranch offered newly built log cabins, majestic views and goat yoga. It seemed the perfect spot to let go of the wedding stress and head into marriage feeling invigorated. So, she decided to have a bachelorette trip with Mercy, Cassady and their longtime friend Nash Landry. They were leaving tomorrow and would spend two weeks of relaxation at Hideaway Ranch before heading home. Then the one-week countdown to the wedding would begin.

Cassady disappeared into the crowd after she and Rowan hugged. Circulating the crowd, Rowan greeted everyone to make them feel welcome and say thank you for coming to celebrate her love with Dutton. At last, the guests found their seats and her bridesmaids and groomsmen were gathered in the church foyer.

"Okay." Rowan's heart was beating too fast, and she felt cold and clammy as the rehearsal was about to begin. "It's go time."

Her mom, on Denver's arm, and Dutton's parents were escorted first to their seats at the front of the church. Then her ten bridesmaids, including Mercy and Cassady, were escorted by Dutton's groomsmen and Nash, and then her father, misty-eyed, led her down the aisle to Dutton.

He was handsome in his own way. Looking rather

dashing in a navy blue suit, Dutton looked at her with a nervous smile and a quivering lip. He was dabbing sweat off his forehead.

"I'm counting on you," her father told Dutton quietly.

"Yes, sir." Dutton shook his hand, a noticeably high-pitched waver in his voice. "I'll try to do my best."

Her father kept hold of Dutton's hand, his serious gaze holding Dutton's eyes like a Spock mind-meld. "I expect you to do your best, not try. Do."

Dutton nodded his head and when her father let go of his hand, he rubbed it. Her dad did have an impressive grip.

Her father kissed Rowan on the cheek and then took his seat by her mother.

"It's okay." Rowan took Dutton's hands in hers. His palms were sweaty, and it was making the tiniest of alarm bells ring in her mind. "I'm nervous, too. That's why we do this. Get the kinks out before our big day."

Her fiancé tugged his hand free and dabbed more sweat off his forehead. Now she was feeling uneasy. The priest began the rehearsal while Dutton pulled on his necktie.

"Is it hot in here?" Dutton asked, making the priest pause.

Embarrassed, Rowan apologized to the priest. Then quietly to Dutton, she asked, "What is going on?"

"I need to talk to you," Dutton whispered, sweat running down his cheeks.

"Now?"

"Right now."

She made their excuses to their guests and then followed Dutton through a door to the room reserved for the groom's party.

Dutton closed the door behind her, and then he ripped off his tie, took a nearby towel and rubbed the sweat off his face.

"What. Is. Going. On?" she asked sternly. "We have nearly a hundred people out there. We both have family in from out of town for this."

Dutton looked her straight in the eye, and it did occur to her that he hadn't done that so much lately. She had thought it was because of the big business deal he was working on in Washington state with his father.

"Rowan. I'm sorry."

Her hands went to her hips. "Don't you dare."

"I can't marry you."

"No."

"I'm..." he started. "I have been..."

Confusion, anger, disbelief and shock were all hitting her smack in the face. "What have you done?"

"I've been seeing someone."

Her eyebrows lowered, and she knew she looked confused because she was. "Like a doctor? Are you sick?"

"I'm going to be a father."

She couldn't get one word out of her mouth.

"Do you get what I'm trying to tell you, Row?"

She slit her eyes at him. "Explain it to me like I'm stupid, Dutton."

"I met someone in Seattle."

"You met someone," she repeated as a compulsion.

"I've fallen in love."

"You've fallen in love."

"And she's pregnant."

Rowan's eyes widened, and she felt sick and dizzy. In a voice that was not her own, she yelled at him, "You got her pregnant? What about not having sex before marriage?"

Mercy and Cassady rushed into the room, and Rowan, without thinking, pointed at Dutton and yelled, "Hit him!"

Chapter One

Thirty-year-old cowboy Axel Redford was letting off some steam with his friends-of-convenience in a honky-tonk in Bozeman, Montana. He had been crashing with a sweet little friends-with-benefits rodeo princess for a week or two, but had to pull up stakes when her sweet turned sour. He could bunk with one of his bar buddies, but he decided to unroll his sleeping bag and get some shut-eye in the back of his truck. It wouldn't be the first time or the last.

"I'm gonna head out." Axel finished his bottle of beer. "My day starts in the dark."

"Man. Don't go," said a wiry guy by the nickname of Priest. "I was just about to win back my fifty."

Axel smiled at him. "Naw, partner. I know when it's quittin' time." He stopped by the bar, fished out his wallet from the back pocket of his faded jeans, peeled off a one-hundred-dollar bill and waited for the bartender to head back his way.

He had eyes in his head, and he surely loved to admire beautiful women. This night, the object of his gaze was a woman with porcelain skin and freckles dusted across her nose and cheeks; those freckles were on her shoulders as well, easy to spot because she was wearing a tight strapless dress that hugged her figure in all the right ways. But what had caught his eye first was the thick, fiery red hair she wore loose and long to the small of her back.

Man. Redheads. They were his downfall. Unfortunately, it was all look and don't touch; this little filly was spoken for, according to the Bride-to-Be sash she wore.

Axel held out the folded bill to the bartender; the bartender nodded his appreciation, and just as Axel turned away from the bar, someone bumped into him. He turned around to find the lovely red-haired bride-to-be.

"No!" she called out in frustration to the bartender who had already moved down to the other end of the bar. "Come back!"

"Can I help you?" Axel asked without any idea why he had just inserted himself into the tipsy woman's life.

She dropped her head and hands down. "I need a whiskey sour."

Axel whistled loudly, waved his hand, and the bartender headed back their way. "An emergency whiskey sour," Axel said.

"Coming right up." The bartender nodded.

The bride-to-be leaned against the bar and smiled up at him. "You're like my knight in shining…" She stopped, looked him up and down, and then said, "I don't see anything shining."

Yes, she was tipsy, but she wasn't sloppy. On her, it was cute. She had lightened his mood without any effort on her part. And darned if she wasn't prettier up close. He'd be tempted to extend his night if she wasn't wearing that sash.

Axel paid for the drink.

"No!" the woman said. "I can't let you pay for my drink."

"Sure, you can," he said easily. "It's my gift to you and your lucky groom."

"Well. Thank you." She took a sip of the drink.

He was fixing to walk away when she added, "He's not lucky."

His ears perked right up, and he hated that he was still playing in her sandbox. "Come again?"

"He's not lucky!" she shouted over the noise.

Now his curiosity got the better of him. With an amused smile, he asked, "Why not?"

She held out her sash for him to read. "Bride *not* to be."

In between the words *bride* and *to*, the word *not* was written in black ink, smeared on the white satin.

"Who the heck let you get away?" he asked.

"Oh," she said with a shake of her head. "It's a whole thing. I'd rather dance."

"I can dance," he volunteered.

A man in his mid-twenties appeared from the crowd. "Rowan," he said. "You okay?"

She nodded, still sipping on her drink. "This guy right here bought me a drink. We're going to dance."

Not wanting to do the three-is-a-crowd deal, Axel asked, "Are you the ex?"

"No. Just a friend." The man held out his hand. "Nash Landry."

Axel shook it. "Axel."

Rowan held up her hand. "Rowan."

"Just a friendly bit of advice." Nash looked at his friend and then back to Axel. "I wouldn't go spinning her if I were you."

Axel's plan for an early night turned into closing down the bar with Rowan and Nash. After the drink he bought for her, Rowan switched to water and kept him busy dancing to every upbeat song the band played. Darn it if he didn't have to switch to water just to keep hydrated with all of the sweating trying to keep up with Rowan. Somewhere along the line, he'd started to nickname her *Spitfire* in his mind.

A slow song came on, and Rowan made a dissatisfied, frustrated noise. She headed back to the booth where Nash was hunkered down against the wall, cowboy hat over his face.

"You know," Axel told Rowan, "I've got some pretty slick slow dance moves."

Rowan pulled a sour expression, shook her head and then headed for the ladies'.

"Is she always the energizer bunny?" Axel asked Nash.

Nash slid his hat back. "Always."

"She's wearing me out."

That made Nash laugh. "She *can* do that."

After a short pause, Axel said carefully, "Sounds like she got a pretty raw deal."

Nash's smile faded, and his jaw tightened. "Man,

I'm telling ya. It was brutal. Nearly the whole damn town was there. Videos and pictures uploaded instantly. People on socials love to build a body up, but they like even better when they can tear them down and drag them through the mud."

Axel said, "Her ex must be a real piece of work."

That was all he had to say for Nash to crack right open. And Nash was still talking when Rowan returned with bottles of water.

"Band only has one more set," she told them. "Are you up for closing the place down?"

Nash chuckled. "If I say no, will that change anything?"

Rowan smiled at her friend, and for the first time, Axel could see the light in her eyes. "Probably not."

"Then we're closing down the place." Nash slid his hat back down to cover his eyes. "Wake me up when it's over."

The band had taken a short break and was now back on the stage. Rowan looked at Axel. "Are you staying or going?"

I should say that I'm going. Early morning, long day of ranching ahead. "Staying."

That earned him the smallest of smiles, and it only made him hungry for more. As he followed Spitfire to the dance floor, Axel began to feel something inside that he hadn't felt in too many years to count. That initial attraction had unexpectedly grown into interest and curiosity. But she was coming off a big breakup. No one was ready for a relationship after that kind of loss.

He'd rebounded with his share of women, and he'd

been on the receiving end of that same scenario himself. It was like a punch to the gut and an uppercut to the chin. He wasn't in a hurry to feel that way again.

On the way back to the dance floor, he crossed paths with one of the acquaintances he'd left at the pool table.

"Did'ya get hooked?" the man teased him.

"Cowpoke, it sure looks that'away."

When the band bid everyone goodnight, Axel walked with Nash and Rowan to the sidewalk just outside the bar. In the streetlight, which was certainly brighter than the bar, Axel could see that Rowan's mascara had bled around her eyes from the sweat. She looked rather like a raccoon. She had tamed her thick red hair into a topknot when they danced, but part of it had fallen, and the rest was plastered to the top of her head with sweat. In all of his days, he'd never seen anyone more attractive than Rowan. It was flat-out odd.

Rowan held out her hand to him. "Thank you for the dancing."

"My pleasure."

"Nice to meet you." Nash held out his hand, as well.

"Same on this side."

They said good-night, and then Axel watched Rowan and Nash walk away together. After she had disappeared from his sight, Axel walked to his truck. Lying flat on his back in the bed of his truck, he replayed the evening.

He didn't know Spitfire's last name. He couldn't remember Nash's. He didn't know if they lived in Bozeman or if they were just visiting. He didn't have any way to contact them. He'd wanted to ask for her number, but he'd been around long enough to know better.

So, he might never see Rowan again. If only he had thought of some way to keep in touch without seeming like a greasy come-on. In his defense, he had been distracted by her eyes.

"Amateur," Axel scolded himself, looking up at the sliver of moon above. "You let that one get away."

"We had two cabins checking out today. Cleaning services will be here this afternoon," Charlotte "Charlie" Brand said to her sisters, Rayna and Danica. They were known in the Big Sky area as the Brand triplets; Rayna and Danica were identical twins while Charlie rounded out the three as the fraternal twin. "And only one arrival."

Charlie Brand was a strong, independent, brave Montana cowgirl. She was born to live the ranch life, and for many years she had held Hideaway Ranch together with only her determination and sheer gumption to hold on to the pristine land settled by her ancestors five generations ago. But the ranch was being held together by a frayed string, and when the pandemic hit, that string broke. Luckily, and possibly through divine intervention, the sisters were able to come back together and work as a team to save Hideaway Ranch.

"Isn't that one of our long-lost relatives?" asked Rayna "Ray" Brand. Ray had been a stay-at-home mom, raising her two sons in Connecticut, playing the role of perfect wife for her high-profile attorney husband, when her husband, seemingly out of the blue, asked for a divorce. The life she had built for nearly twenty years was over, and the only place she could think to lick her wounds and regroup was her childhood home: Hideaway Ranch. The idea of romance was the last thing on her mind until she ran into her first love, single father Dean Legend, and when those sparks started to fly again, Ray's fears of a lonely life were washed away by Dean's love and devotion.

"Coming out of the woodwork," said Danica "Danny" Brand. Danny was the consummate businesswoman and had built a multimillion-dollar business as the number one realtor to the rich and famous in California. After her longtime business partner and fiancé Grant had announced that their office manager, Fallon, was pregnant with his child, and suggested a path forward as a thruple, Danny cut ties with Grant and went home to Hideaway Ranch. Lady Love was on her side, too, because Danny met the most eligible bachelor in the county, Dr. Matteo Katz. In the snap of a finger, Danny became his fiancée and a mother to a pampered pig by the name of Lu-Lu.

Ray, a softhearted dreamer, said, "Aww. I love it! Here we thought we were alone in the world, and now we are finding family everywhere!"

"Only because our ancestor was a prolific bigamist." Danny tucked some strands of her sleek platinum blond hair behind her ear—an ear adorned with a fiery pink-and-white pig face with two round black diamond eyes. "But if it brings revenue to our ranch, bring on the long-lost Brands."

"Is there such a thing as a trigamist? Or a quadra-mist?" Ray asked, pouring a second round of strong coffee for them. "I think he had more than two wives. Rowan hails from Wyoming."

"Speaking of Rowan," Danny said, "let's get back on track. Anything new there?"

"Actually, yes," Charlie said after a sip of coffee. "This isn't a bachelorette trip anymore."

"What?" Ray's brows drew together.

"Why not?" Danny asked.

"Her fiancé broke up with her during their rehearsal dinner," Charlie said.

Ray's deep blue eyes welled up. "Oh no! That poor girl."

"Ray. Please," Danny said. "Can we manage to get through a state of the ranch meeting without tears? Last week, one of the horses got a summer sore on its lip, and you would swear one of us had died with all the tissues you ran through."

"She's sensitive," Charlie defended Ray. "She must have gotten ours because neither of us is exactly touchy-feely."

Danny contemplated and then agreed, "True."

"So, Rowan didn't cancel. I guess this is a 'thank God I dodged the bullet' trip," Charlie said. "She extended her stay for another week."

Danny nodded. "As long as the card is good and we have the availability."

"Yes to both," Charlie said. "She'll be checking in around noon with Nash and Mercy. Cassady Abbot will be joining in at the beginning of next week. We'll send a car service to the airport for her."

"Well." Danny sighed, typing on her laptop. "It goes against Hideaway's brand of *love is always in bloom* and *romance is always in season*. But she is a cousin eighteen million times removed. So, I suppose I can make an exception."

"Look at that, Ray!" Charlie teased. "Danny's going soft on us."

"Oh, I hope so. And you never know." Ray's expression said her mind was full of the possibilities that could unfold for Rowan. "Maybe Rowan will find love here. It happened to all of us!"

"True," Charlie agreed. "Hideaway Ranch does have a secret sauce."

Hideaway Ranch had brought each of the triplets fiancés, which had anchored the sisters to their legacy ranch. Working together, they had turned their once embattled cattle ranch into a destination bed-and-breakfast. Hideaway Ranch had already inspired marriage, vow renewals, engagements and even a baby. It wouldn't be unheard of if Rowan Brand did find love on this magical land.

"Well." Danny closed her laptop. "I wouldn't mind adding another win in our column." In charge of all of the finances and marketing, Danny had put a romance counter on the website. Potential clients could see that, even though the megamillion-dollar, glitz and glamour rental houses erected around Big Sky Ski Resort offered luxury beyond belief, they couldn't bring them lasting love. But Hideaway Ranch could.

"Are we good here?" Danny asked, putting her laptop in her designer bag. "It's time for Lu-Lu's walk. She's put on some pounds."

Ray and Charlie exchanged a look, and then Ray said, "She's a pig."

Danny slung her bag over her shoulder. "And?"

Charlie said, "She's a pig."

"Look." Danny pointed at each of them in turn. "Ray, you handle your goat yoga goats, Charlie, you handle your horses and let me take care of my fabulous Lu-Lu."

Rowan was hungover. Even though she had traded water for whiskey halfway through the night, her head hurt, and she felt dehydrated and gross. She could still smell the scent of stale beer on her clothes and the soles of her boots were sticky. Nash was behind the wheel of their rental car, and Mercy was sitting in the front seat. Rowan was gratefully in the back seat, seat belt stretched to its limit so she could slump over and put her head on a pillow she had brought from home.

"We have arrived!" Nash bellowed like an announcer for WrestleMania.

Mercy covered her ears. "Nash! Seriously?"

Rowan sat up and then had to close her eyes against the dizziness. "You need to tone that down."

"Sorry."

Once she felt steady enough to open her eyes, Rowan was immediately grateful to Nash for forcing her to sit up and take note. As they drove along the gravel drive that had some dips and potholes from snow and rain, she breathed in and felt a shift inside of her body.

What was this? Yes, the ranch was even more beautiful in person, but wasn't that true with most places? Could this land have what she needed to heal her broken heart? Time would tell.

Nash drove up to the main cabin, the hub and heartbeat of Hideaway Ranch, both nostalgic and beautiful. A large newly painted barn was to the left, and next to that was a building with a sign that read The Everything Barn. An inviting firepit was surrounded by several log seats, no doubt harvested from the ranch. Straight ahead were sweeping pastures with tall grass swaying gently in the afternoon breeze and a herd of horses, heads down and tails swishing at flies.

It was picturesque, but not all that different from Wyoming. But again, Rowan felt something in her body switch on, as quickly as one could switch on a light. It was both unsettling and curious.

"Welcome to Hideaway Ranch!"

Two women came out of the main house to greet them. One had sun-flushed cheeks, tanned skin and deeply grooved lines at the corner of her eyes, silvery hair pulled back in a simple braid down her back, well-worn denim jeans and a broad smile. The other woman had auburn hair twisted up in a topknot held together by what looked to be a pen. Her jeans were dark-washed and neat, her glasses round, her blue eyes so clear, and her smile open and warm.

"I'm Charlie." The cowgirl with a ruddy complexion introduced herself.

The second woman put her hand over her heart and said, "And I'm Ray."

"Now!" Charlie rested her hands at her waist. "Who's our long-lost kin?"

Rowan recognized them from their website and socials. Yes, her head still hurt, her mouth felt like she had been eating Elmer's glue, and she was generally feeling devastated. But Charlie with her bold appearance, and Ray with her positive aura, made her feel a smidge better.

"That would be me." Rowan held up her hand.

Charlie and Ray rushed to her for a double hug. Rowan could actually feel their unconditional acceptance of her as family, no matter how many times removed.

"We are so happy to meet you," Ray said, her eyes swimming with tears.

Charlie must have read the concern on Rowan's face. She pulled a wad of tissues out of her back pocket and handed them to Ray. "Don't pay any mind to those tears."

"Happy tears." Ray dabbed her eyes.

"She cries at anything, for any reason, at any time," Charlie said.

"Aw," Rowan said in unison with Mercy. She felt compelled to hug Ray, so she did. "Thank you for such a wonderful welcome."

"Thank you," Ray said and then turned to Charlie. "See? She gets it."

Rowan introduced Nash and Mercy to their hosts. When introductions were done, Charlie said, "Well, no sense chewing the fat. Let's get you settled into your cabin so you can get started with what I am certain will be a trip to remember."

In her own mind, Rowan said, *I hope this is a trip that will help me forget.*

Once in their cabin, fatigue from her life set in. All she wanted to do was sleep so she could stop replaying the events that had unfolded at the rehearsal dinner. No matter how badly she wanted to reach out to Dutton, she stopped herself. There were so many questions in her mind. Perhaps it was best that they weren't answered; knowing was often worse than imagining what might have happened.

Rowan told her friends that she would be taking a nap. She shut the door to her room, left her suitcase unpacked and face-planted on the bed. Burying her face in her favorite pillow, she groaned. It was still difficult to accept what had happened. She was in shock, she supposed.

And the response on her socials was rather horrific. People could be brutal online, and her humiliation had emboldened the barracudas lurking in the slimy underbelly of social media. It was like being stabbed, killed, then brought back to life only to be stabbed in the heart again.

In full-on wallowing, Rowan thought she heard a knock on the front door, but she ignored it. Then, she heard Mercy calling out to her.

"Hey, Row?"

"Whaat-tuh?" she yelled so she could be heard through the pillow.

"Did you order a cowboy?"

Chapter Two

"Did I order a cowboy?" Rowan thought for a minute, rolled over onto her back and swiped at the hair stuck to her cheeks. "What the heck does that mean?"

She scooted to the edge of the bed, then walked to the door, opened it and went to a railing that gave her a bird's-eye view of the living room and the front door.

There, in the doorway, was Axel.

He lifted up his hat as a show of respect and waved to her. "Hey there." The backcountry drawl sent a lovely tingle racing up her spine right to the pleasure centers of the brain.

"Hi," she said, managing a less-than-welcoming tone. She pinched her eyebrows together for good measure.

"I'm Axel."

"I know." She crossed her arms in front of her body. "Why are you here? How did you find me? *Why* did you find me?"

Mercy's head was on a swivel, bouncing back and forth between the two of them. "Axel, I'm Mercy."

Axel lifted his cowboy hat and reached out to shake

her friend's hand before replacing his hat on his head. "Nice to meet you, Mercy."

Cowboy charm. I've fallen for that my whole entire life. Look where it's gotten me.

"Do you want to come in? It's starting to heat up out there," Mercy quipped. "And in here, apparently."

"Thank you kindly." Axel stepped over the threshold.

Now Rowan's dander was up. In her bare feet, and with what she knew was a disheveled appearance, she took the stairs quickly and walked with intention over to the cowboy and Mercy. Arms still crossed, she asked, "Why are you here?"

She'd had a good time dancing with Axel until they shut down the bar. And that was it. She'd never expected to see him again, and she was fine with that. Cowboys like Axel were bad news. They'd leave a trail of broken hearts as they headed out of town. And she'd already had enough heartbreak.

"Would you like some water?" Mercy continued with the niceties expected of a young lady hailing from anywhere in Wyoming. "We also have soda."

Mercy always had a way of making every stranger feel like one of the family. But at this moment, Rowan didn't want this cowboy to feel like one of the family.

"Mercy?" She gave her dear friend a look. "We aren't entertaining him."

Her friend mouthed the word *sorry* to Axel. He gave her a nod of understanding, as if the two of them had a special code just between them. And somehow, Rowan was the one who was being rude.

"I work here," Axel answered her question at last.

"You work *here*?" Rowan repeated. "*Here*, here?"

"Yes."

"Oh, that's nice." Mercy always tried to look on the bright side. "You already have a friend."

Rowan breathed in long and deep, head lowered, before she exhaled and said to Mercy, "Would you please give us just a moment?"

"Oh!" Mercy exclaimed as if it just occurred to her that something weird was going down. "Of course." Her friend gave a nod and a smile. "It was a pleasure to meet you, Axel."

"Likewise."

"And I'm sure we will see you around," Mercy said, not really moving.

"Well, I bet you could count on that."

"Mercy," Rowan said. "Please. I'm sorry. I love you. I have a migraine, and you're making it worse."

Mercy nodded quietly and now Rowan felt like a horrible person for hurting the feelings of her highly sensitive and emotional dear friend. When her friend disappeared into the kitchen, Rowan leaned in and whispered harshly, "Now look what you did! You're already causing trouble."

"What did *I* do?" Axel asked with what she read as genuine surprise.

"Please," she said, "you know. You show up here with your pretty face and those ridiculous biceps and your aw-shucks drawl, so used to women dropping like flies at your feet."

"I wouldn't necessarily call my face pretty."

Her hands went to her hips. *"That's* what you're zeroing in on?"

"I'm glad to see you."

"How did you even know I'm here?"

"Look," Axel said, "Charlie told me a guest named Rowan Brand, kin to them, had just checked in, and to go introduce myself to you, but I had a feeling we had already met."

Wordlessly, she frowned at him, arms crossed.

"We had a good time." Axel smiled at her with a Tom Cruise–style crooked grin that made him very appealing, and therefore to her, even more annoying.

"Yes. We did," she acknowledged. "And I never expected to see you again."

"Well, I'm here." Axel took a small step closer to her, as if testing how far he could go before she gave him an uppercut to that cleft chin of his. "Why can't we keep on having fun?"

She stared at him, and he stared right back at her with a questioning eyebrow raise. This cowboy was good-looking in a gritty sort of way, and she could tell he knew how to show a cowgirl a good time. Perhaps she was due for a rebound romance? Keep it light with a cowboy who no doubt pulled stakes when the whim struck. "Actually, I can't think of any reason why not."

He tilted his head to the side and sent her a slight smile. "Ride out at daybreak? See the sunrise?"

"Don't you have to work?"

"I'm workin'," Axel said. "Charlie told me you wanted to explore the ranch on horseback. I'm the ranch guide now. Meet me in the horse barn at daybreak?"

"Okay. Fine," she said, opening the door behind him.

He stepped outside, turned and gave her his cowboy salutation, hat tipped at the brim. Before he was finished, she shut the door.

Axel walked back to the bunkhouse, feeling like he'd just got hit over the head with a hammer. Man. Rowan Brand. When she came down those stairs, fire in her eyes, her mane of hair tangled and her mascara smudged, something in his heart got wrenched open. Damn. Spitfire.

"Damn," he repeated. He'd known heartbreak. Rowan was dangerous. His sense of connection with her, the chemistry that had kept him dancing until well after midnight, was undeniable. But he had to face the facts. Rowan came with a boatload of baggage. He felt drawn to her, almost compelled to spend more time with her even knowing that this could end on a lousy note for him.

"Hey, Axel." Nash was sitting on one of the top bunk beds. The room was pretty full; the Brand triplets had learned to jump on the projects for the ranch right when the ground began to melt. Many of the workers—carpenters, painters and cowhands—needed a place to get shut-eye. That place was the recently refurbished bunkhouse.

Axel hung up his hat on the post of his bunk bed. "Not staying with the girls?"

Nash sat up, dangled his legs off the side of the frame. "Nah. They're my crew, I love them, but three women under one roof? That's too much estrogen for my taste."

Axel laughed. He already liked Nash. "Want coffee?" he asked, heading to the kitchenette situated along one wall of the bunkhouse.

"Sure." Nash hopped down and walked over to the small dining table with a book still in his hand.

"What are you reading?" Axel asked after getting the coffee brewing.

Nash showed him the cover of the book.

"'Paleontology,'" Axel read the title aloud. "Summer reading?"

That made Nash laugh. "I wouldn't have predicted that hunting dinosaur fossils would be my path. But I love it."

Axel leaned back. "How'd that go?"

Nash put the book down. "Money."

"Yeah, buddy."

"Wyoming is like Montana. Cattle was how our family scratched out a living."

Axel nodded.

"My family couldn't compete with the mega ranchers like the Brands. Calf prices have tanked. When folks with big cattle are feeling the pinch? Our ranch goes under."

Axel grabbed some cups of coffee for them, and they fixed their coffee to taste.

Nash took a sip and then laughed. "That's pure mud!"

Axel laughed with a smile. "Ain't it, though?" Then

he nodded to the book Nash had been reading. "What's a dinosaur have to do with the price of cattle?"

"Wyoming is full of dinosaur fossils, man. No joke. Our neighbors have hit the jackpot with a T. rex with all of the bones."

"Are you serious?"

Nash nodded. "We found a mammoth tusk and the skull of a triceratops."

"What's that look like?"

His new bunkmate flipped through the book and then turned it around to show a picture of the massive dinosaur.

"How do you even find something like that?"

"They're just pushing up to the surface. They've been hidden for twenty-six million years, and if you know what to look for, you can find them."

Axel whistled. "What's the money in that?"

"It depends on the market really. Five years ago, a T. rex skeleton named Stan sold for thirty-two million."

Axel drained his coffee and set it down on the table. "Thirty-two million? That's some walking around money."

"Yeah. The money is the object. We've got bills long overdue. But I love the hunt," Nash said. "And I'm good at it. I haven't been much of a cowboy. But I can find fossils. Even big ranchers like Rowan's family are getting into the game." He gave his head a shake. "You put your hands on something that's been hidden for millions of years… It's a rush. It's frickin' amazing."

Axel liked Nash—he seemed like a good guy. The fact that he was Rowan's friend might be handy along the way. He just couldn't think of a segue from dinosaurs to Rowan. Segues weren't his strength. "Speaking of amazing," he began. The moment after he opened his mouth, he felt like an idiot.

Nash shook his head with a sigh of resignation. "You've caught it."

"Caught what?"

"Whatever happens to men when they see Rowan," Nash said. "A virus that causes over-the-top romantic gestures, professions of love and really embarrassing poetry read aloud to captive audiences, of which I have been a member more times than I care to recall."

Axel took a minute to absorb what Nash had just told him.

"Can I give you some unsolicited advice that you will not heed?" Nash asked.

"Sure."

"No matter how many men have thrown themselves at Rowan's feet, her heart has only belonged to Dutton since we were kids. He was the popular kid, she was not. Totally unrequited for her. Then, one day, she went on a double date with Mercy and her boyfriend, and Rowan finally caught her big fish."

Before Axel could respond, Wayne Westbrook, Charlie Brand's fiancé and ranch foreman, appeared in the doorway. Wayne whistled at him and waved his hand for him to follow. Because Wayne could make or break his time at Hideaway, Axel got up quick and followed his boss.

His body was turned to the work ahead, but his mind was soup. Nash didn't seem to be trying to throw him off Rowan's scent; he just seemed like a guy who was giving him an insider perspective. Would he heed it? Nope.

But did the information help? It sure did.

"Oh." Rowan sat on the comfy couch in the vaulted family room. Mercy had brought her a cool compress for her head. "Thank you."

Mercy sat down at the other end, one leg curled underneath her. Her very sweet face, always filled with hope and kindness, added curiosity to that list.

"I was mean to him," Rowan said with self-admonishment. "I'll apologize."

"Who is he to you?"

"Nobody."

"He's somebody."

With a sigh, Rowan took the compress off her head. "I met him in a bar, and we danced. I had no idea he worked here."

"Hmm."

Rowan pushed herself up. "That's a loaded *hmm*."

Mercy tucked a couple of strands of honey blond hair behind her ear. "I..." her dear friend started, then stopped.

"Mercy. Just say it," Rowan said. "We've always had space in our friendship to tell the truth. What's on your mind?"

Mercy nodded. Then she said, "I don't want to see you rush into something. Axel doesn't seem like the kind of guy who's able to commit."

"That's what I like about him," Rowan explained. "I

didn't know he was going to be here. But he is. Why shouldn't I have some harmless fun while I'm trying to dislodge that knife Dutton rammed into my heart?"

"Oh." Mercy reached out to put her hand on Rowan's arm. "Gosh, Row. I'm so sorry."

"It's hardly your fault."

Mercy had expressed to her that she carried guilt because she was the one who first suggested they go out as a foursome after Dutton had been dumped by his first love. As it turned out, Rowan was the rebound relationship.

Mercy scooted over to her and wrapped her arms around her. Rowan leaned her head against her friend's and closed her eyes.

"I hate what he did," Mercy said, emotion in her voice.

"I know you do," Rowan said. "But you need to get over that. I don't blame you. All I care about is that your relationship with Doug doesn't become collateral damage in this mess."

Mercy leaned back so she could meet her gaze. "And *our* relationship doesn't become collateral damage."

"Yes. Of course. One hundred percent."

"Promise me, Row."

"I promise."

Mercy seemed satisfied with that answer, but Rowan wasn't so sure how it would all work out. For sure she would be seeing Dutton at important events for Mercy and Doug. They were already engaged, and a date had been set for the following year. How would she feel the first time she saw Dutton? How would she feel the first time she saw him with his baby and the mother of their child? Sick. Horribly, unbelievably, majorly sick.

"I just want you to know, Mercy." Rowan put her hand over her friend's. "If I can have a good time with Axel, and it takes my mind off the fallout from this small-town scandal, I'm going to do it."

"Okay." Mercy nodded pensively. "Just don't go giving your heart away."

Rowan made a cross over her heart. "Not a chance."

Axel liked to be alone. In the main horse barn was a small office tucked away at the back of the tack room. He had never seen anyone use it, so he had taken to going there when he needed to get away. After his work was done and Wayne had told him to call it a day, Axel borrowed one of Nash's dinosaur books and settled into the office to read. Something about the idea of cowboys hunting for fossils intrigued him.

"Hi, sweet baby." A woman's voice drifted in from where some of the horses were bedded down at night.

Axel closed his book and listened very carefully. *Rowan?* He left the office and walked out of the tack room. Sure enough, there was Rowan, petting a giant Percheron mare named Phoenix.

"Howdy."

Rowan startled, hand on her chest, and then she laughed. "You caught me off guard. Good thing I have a strong heart."

He leaned against a wall, just admiring Rowan's beauty. She was curvy, and her red hair loose and flowing around her shoulders and down her back made a perfect frame for her lovely heart-shaped face.

"You decided to skip the campfire tonight," he said.

Rowan turned her attention from the loving mare, met his gaze and walked toward him.

Inside, he felt nervous. He wasn't typically nervous around women; he liked women, he was close to his two older sisters, and he counted several hearty women as his best friends back in Kentucky.

"I feel like I was rude to you earlier," she said. "I'm sorry for that. Not my usual."

"You don't owe me a darn thing," he said. "You've been through it."

She rolled her eyes a bit. "True story."

There was an uncomfortable silence, and then Rowan nearly blew him off his feet with her next statement.

"You want to kiss me."

She didn't pose it as a question because they both knew it was a fact.

He swallowed hard several times, trying to pry his tongue loose from the roof of his mouth. In his experience with women, not one of them had studied him like he was a filet mignon. "I've thought about it a time or two."

"You know I'm heartbroken. You saw the Bride Not to Be sash."

He nodded.

"You know this is mostly a rebound situation."

"Yes. I've done the math."

"Still, you don't seem like a man who sticks around too long."

He looked at the toe of his boot. "I've moved around a bit."

"A good-time cowboy, woman in every port kind of deal."

Rowan's estimate of him was wrong. But his grandpa had taught him that it was always the right time to keep his mouth zipped.

"I like you," Rowan said.

"I like you."

"You're obviously handsome."

"You're obviously beautiful."

A flash of pain entered her striking blue eyes, but then it vanished. But not before he could see it.

"So, we agree right here and now that we are just having a good time." Rowan took another step toward him, close enough for that kiss she had mentioned. "No strings."

"No strings."

"Just a good time while it lasts."

He nodded.

Rowan stood up on tiptoe, put her hands on his face and then kissed him. And that kiss sent a shock wave through his body. The scent of her hair, the feel of her cool hands on his face, the softness of her full lips…

When the kiss was over, he looked down into Rowan's face to see if she had been similarly moved by their first kiss, but all he saw were the shutters she had pulled down over her eyes, hiding the windows to her soul.

"Sunrise?" she asked.

"Here at sunrise."

Rowan bid him good-night and left him alone with his conflicted thoughts.

There was already a chance that he was in over his head with the pretty, bold redhead. Not enough to scare him off. Then again, he could be real stubborn, and he didn't scare easy.

Rowan held her composure until she reached the outside of the barn. She was in the shadows, hidden from sight. She leaned back against the barn, closed her eyes and tried to catch her breath.

That kiss had knocked her for a loop. Never in her life had she felt a spark like that. Not with Dutton. Not with anyone. The scent of his skin, the feel of his lips on hers… The natural electricity between them… That couldn't be manufactured or changed. It just *was*.

"Tread lightly, Row," she said as she made her way back to the cabin.

There was a very good chance that she was getting in over her head with this smoking-hot cowboy. She didn't need to blindly jump from the pan into the fire. And with Axel Redford? There was nothing *but* fire.

Chapter Three

Rowan was up before dawn. She rolled out of bed and got dressed quickly. She braided her hair into one large, thick braid down her back. She pulled on jeans that would fit over her boots and some half chaps to keep her inner thighs from being pinched by the stirrup straps. She also had a helmet. Many ranchers still chose to ride without a helmet, but Rowan had a friend who had a severe concussion from a fall off a horse, and it had made her wary. She had been in the saddle from the time she was a toddler; she didn't care how many years she had clocked on horseback. It only took one accident to ruin a life.

Downstairs, she made herself a quick cup of coffee; the Brand triplets had stocked the fridge with all of her favorite things, right down to her must-have creamer. The coffee was a chaser for her piece of toast with avocado, and then she headed out the door. She was going to be riding with Axel today, and she couldn't lie to herself and pretend she wasn't feeling a lift in her spirits. And she particularly liked the fact that this flirtation between them had a definite shelf life. After her time at Hideaway Ranch, it would be game over for their summer romance.

"Good morning," she said to Axel, who was tacking up a red-and-white Appaloosa mare.

"Mornin'," Axel said with an easy smile that made her smile in return.

"Wow!" she said to the mare. "Aren't you a beauty?"

"She's a looker."

Rowan ran her hand along the mare's sleek neck. "White horse with dark spots over the entire body. You're a leopard."

Axel stopped and looked at her. "You know your horses."

"I do." She nodded. "What's your name, lovely?"

"Aquarius."

"I like that," she said. "I wonder about the origin story."

"Well." Axel tightened the girth slightly, letting the mare adjust her breath before he cinched it tighter. "If you look right here on her rump, you can see all of the points of the Aquarius constellation."

Rowan moved to the mare's hind quarters, watching Axel touch the spots that, when taken as a whole, did in fact form the Aquarius constellation she had pulled up on her phone. "Who in the world figured that one out?"

"Charlie," he said. "This little beauty came with the name Spotsy."

Rowan scrunched up her nose. "Terrible."

"Yep."

"Well, then I'm even more impressed with my ten-times-removed cousin."

That made Axel laugh, and just like when he smiled, she smiled, when he laughed, she laughed. For whatever reason, and she had no reason to analyze it, she felt better when she was with Axel. With him, she was completely free of the drama she would be mired in after this trip. Even with her friend group, Mercy was engaged to Dutton's best friend, Doug. Now that the betrayal had played out publicly, privately there was an awkwardness between her childhood friend and her. Something that had never happened between them. Heck, the worst fight they had ever had was over a Barbie dress. Now? The stakes were off the Richter scale. This wasn't playing in the sandbox. This was real life, and it was going to get real messy until everyone found a new equilibrium.

It was still dark when Rowan and Axel rode out. Most of her riding experience had been on the flat plains of Wyoming. The landscape could feel monotonous with the horizon always looking the same. Fun for galloping full-tilt but not for much else. Yes, there were many interesting rock formations, but it still had a desert feel. Here in Big Sky, Rowan immediately saw what drew her to Hideaway in the first place. She wanted to ride up into the mountains, surrounded by old trees with sprawling canopies. She wanted to stand at the top of a mountain and survey her surroundings.

The fact that Hideaway was owned by her triplet cousins only solidified her draw to this land. A trip that was meant to ground her, refresh her before the wedding, had turned into a heart-healing trip.

"She hasn't missed a step," Rowan said of her mount.

It was dark with hardly any stars in the sky and a sliver of moon that didn't cast off any light to see the way forward. But horses had decent night vision, so she had to put her faith in this pretty little Appaloosa. She wanted adventure and fun, and that was what she was getting right from the jump.

"She knows this trail."

They rode in silence for a while, reaching a forest. The limbs of the trees appeared as long, twisted limbs of a sorcerer, and the leaves crunched beneath the hooves of their horses. It all felt magical. Aquarius made the occasional snort to clear her airway, then bobbed her head several times. Every now and again, the mare would reach out for a tasty bunch of leaves. Even the sound of Aquarius chewing was food for Rowan's soul.

Axel halted his horse, swung his right leg over the horse's hindquarters and dismounted. "We'll walk them up from here."

"Okay."

Rowan dismounted as well, took the reins over the mare's head so she could lead the horse along as they walked up a steep rocky hill that was slippery from a light rain the night before. At the top of the hill, they tied the horses to a tree that would allow them to eat succulent leaves and then take a nap when they had enough.

The sky was changing from inky black to inky blue; Rowan could see the sun beginning to peek over the mountain on the other side of a large valley. Together, they found a perch and sat down to watch the sun begin to rise.

"Water?" he asked her.

"Sure. Thanks."

She twisted off the top of the bottle, took a long draw, then screwed the cap back on. She sat with her knees bent so she could wrap her arms around them. She was aware of Axel, of course. He smelled fantastic. But she did her best to stay focused on the daily miracle unfolding before her. In a way, this moment, this sunrise, marked the beginning of a new chapter in her life.

She breathed in deeply and let it out on a long sigh. The first rays of gold pushed up behind the mountain ridges, then slowly revealed themselves, nature's way of showing off to those who were paying attention.

Beside her, Axel seemed equally as enthralled. Moment by moment, the sun sent wondrous rays of light across the valley, touching their faces with the warmth of the early-morning sun.

"Wow," she said.

Axel looked at her profile, but she just kept on basking in the warm glow. She tilted her head back, closing her eyes, and then sent a prayer to the heavens for a quick healing of her broken heart.

She had tossed and turned all night, playing back the last couple of months with Dutton. Had he been distant? Had he been secretive? Had she missed signs because she trusted him completely? She was aware that dwelling on all that wasn't helpful to her healing. But she couldn't seem to stop. She had even engaged in some late-night social media snooping. That was when she'd first been confronted by a picture of Dutton and a very classy, fashionable, willowy woman who had to be the mother of his child.

How could that be? How could anyone, other than her, be the mother of Dutton's children?

"Penny for your thoughts?" Axel broke her free from her loop of negative thoughts.

"Not worth a penny."

"Do you want to ride down to the valley below? Take the long way back?"

"Sounds good."

They returned to their horses, untied them and walked them out to a flat area suitable for safe mounting. Before she swung into the saddle, she noticed a nearby tree with thick bark that had seen hundreds of years. There, carved into its deep crevices, was a large heart with initials in the center.

"Who are they?" she wondered aloud.

"Butch and Rose Brand."

"Oh," she said. "The triplets' parents."

"I love how you call them the triplets as if they're one organism."

That made her laugh. "Until I get to know them better, I'm afraid that's how I see them."

"Boy, buddy." He swung into the saddle. "They are different. No doubt about that one."

Rowan mounted, as well. "Look! There are initials carved in this tree, too."

"Charlie and Wayne, Danny and Matteo, Ray and Dean, and Ritza and Lane."

"Who's Ritza?"

"A close family friend," Axel said. "She belongs to Phoenix."

"For a minute there, I thought you were going to say another long-lost Brand. There was a whole lotta funny business going on in the Brand family."

They laughed easily together as they walked the horses slowly down from the ridge to a valley of flowers.

Rowan felt lighter. Happier. Freer. And it did occur to her that even before Dutton had confessed to the infidelity, she hadn't laughed in a long while. She didn't feel it now exactly. But there was a real possibility that she had dodged a bullet with Dutton. Had she ever truly felt happy with him? Or was she trying to fit herself into his life when, in truth, she was that square peg trying her best to fit in the Grange family's rigid, unbending, no-frills-allowed hole?

Axel hated to end the morning with Rowan, but he did take it as a good sign that, just as she was leaving the barn, she turned back to look at him with a cheeky smile on her lovely face. It hadn't taken him long to understand that this woman was as tough as American steel with a kind heart to boot. That combination was nearly impossible to find. Here she was, a day or two after that kind heart of hers had been shattered, actively forcing herself to move on.

That was what the kiss had been for. He knew that. If she kissed him, that was a symbol of her taking her life back. At this point, he didn't give a rat's wazoo the reason behind the kiss. All he knew was that when she kissed him, soft lips, smelling all kinds of good, that brief kiss had short-circuited his brain and lit up all over his body to his singed toes.

"Hey, Axel!"

"Hey."

Charlie was the triplet that he meshed with the best. He liked them all, that was for sure. But Charlie, with her tattered faded cowgirl hat, banged-up boots, overalls and silver hair down to the small of her back just read to him as *badass cowgirl*.

"How was the ride?"

"Good." He nodded. "Good enough that she would like an encore tomorrow."

Charlie gave him a thumbs-up. "Have you seen my better half go through here?"

"No."

One hand at her waist, Charlie frowned down at her phone. "Darn it."

"Anything I can help with?"

Charlie was texting Wayne, no doubt, but sometimes reception would drop off in the higher altitudes. "Yes," she said, sliding her phone into her bib. "Actually, you can. We have a herd of miniature cows arriving in a few weeks."

He squinted his eyes and replayed in his mind what he thought his boss had just said, but finally landed on, "Miniature cows?"

Charlie threw up her hands. "You heard right. I swear Ray is deliberately trying to drive me nuts. I love her like a sister."

That turn of phrase made him chuckle, since Ray *was* her sister.

"But it seems like every year we agree to hold off on adding any manure makers onto the ranch, just for a bit. We have the goats and the chickens and the donkeys. We don't need miniature cows right now."

"Does one ever need a miniature cow?" he asked with a smile.

"Do not say that to Ray," Charlie warned him. "If you do, you will be trapped for an hour while Ray tells you the history, the types, the uses, the God-mandated need for miniature cows in everyone's life."

"Good note," he said with a nod.

"Okay." She pulled out her phone again. "Wayne is going to meet me at the west pasture. Do you want to join?"

"Sure."

Charlie spun on her heel and marched toward the pasture.

"Hey, Charlie."

She stopped and looked back at him with raised eyebrows.

"Would you mind if I spent a little extra time with Rowan?" He coughed, the inside of his mouth suddenly dry as a desert. "Not on the clock."

A knowing glint was in Charlie's blue eyes. "Your time off the clock is your business." She turned away, then spun back around again and pointed at him. "Do not breathe a word of this to Danny. Lord! She will have you writing a testimony for the website to offer more proof that Hideaway Ranch is where love is always in season."

"Duly noted."

Charlie headed out again. And darn it if Axel didn't have to quicken his pace to keep up with his boss. Brand women did not play.

"Good morning!" Rowan walked into the cabin to find two of her besties hanging out in the kitchen. "Coffee smells good!" She gave Nash a hug and then did the same to Mercy.

"Did you kiss and make up?" Mercy asked, handing her a cup of coffee after having poured just the right amount for her. They just knew each other that well.

Rowan smiled. "Yes." *In more ways than one.* But there was no reason at all to share the quick peck in the barn. "You guys have to come with me tomorrow." She sat down at the table with them.

"Crack of dawn?" Mercy wrinkled her pert nose. "No thank you."

"You come from Wyoming stock," Nash said to Mercy. "Up before dawn is the very first line in the job description."

"Luckily, I didn't interview for that job. I want to be a mom first and ranch support staff second."

There was an odd silence between them. Rowan noticed it, diagnosed it, then said, "Do not get all weird about talking about anything with me."

"I just didn't think," Mercy apologized anyway. She was very sensitive and really beat herself up if she almost hurt someone's feelings.

Rowan put her hand on Mercy's arm. "Seriously. I'm okay. We're okay."

"Okay," Mercy said in a less-than-convincing voice.

"I saw her," Rowan told her friends.

"Who?" Nash asked.

"Oooh." Mercy zeroed in on her face.

"Yes." Rowan nodded.

"Who?" Nash asked again.

"The baby mama," Rowan said. "I used every tool in the box to hunt her down and kept right on looking until the pain of looking became too great."

"What's she like?" Clearly, Mercy was simultaneously dying of curiosity and wanting to shut down this entire avenue of questioning.

Rowan understood. "Beautiful. Accomplished. Mensa member. I totally hate her."

"No, you don't," Mercy said.

"No, I don't," Rowan agreed. "Actually, and I am not throwing shade here, I was wondering why she took a step down for Dutton. She's next level. A total boss."

"Ouch," Nash said. "But I'd have to agree there. Mensa member? She's in the top two percent on a standardized test? Did Dutton even graduate high school?"

"He was at our graduation," Mercy pointed out.

"That doesn't mean a thing. With the clout his family holds? Dutton graduating when he didn't have enough credits to graduate? Child's play."

"True." Rowan nodded. "The Granges had just donated a big ol' chunk of cash for the high school to build a state-of-the-art gym."

"Fishy." Mercy nodded.

Then Rowan shook her head to stop letting the Dutton drama rent space in her head. "I'm sick of this topic."

"Same," Mercy said.

"God, yes," Nash agreed.

"Who is up for goat yoga?" she asked her friends.

Mercy was a shoo-in. Loved anything healthy and fun.

"Pass." Nash was an expected no.

"Nash," Rowan said. "You can't sit in your room on our vacay reading about beings that lived two hundred million years ago."

"I think you are mixing *can't* with *shouldn't*."

Rowan walked around the table, took his hand and tugged on it. "Come on, Nash. Remember, I'm brokenhearted and need all the support I can get."

"At all times," Mercy added, picking up their cups and putting them in the sink.

"You actually went there." Nash tried to look annoyed but couldn't. "Isn't it too early to play that card?"

"No," Rowan and Mercy said in unison.

"It's an infinite card," Rowan added. "It never runs out."

"Lord give me strength." Nash shook his head.

And that was that. The three of them headed over to the new yoga studio.

Rowan felt lighter for having seen that sunrise with Axel. She had started to notice that being with Axel helped her keep her mind in Montana, not in Wyoming or in her life on her socials. She liked that about him. She surely did. It didn't hurt at all that he was fine to look at.

* * *

Axel could not get Rowan off his mind. She was a puzzle to him; she was a woman on the surface, but a jumble of contrasting parts down deep. She was playful and funny but also desperately sad. She was strong and commanding but deeply wounded. And he was on the hook. No way around it. He had fallen fast for the redheaded, smoking hot, feisty as all get-out Rowan Brand.

He knew this was a bad place to land. Heartbroken women were a huge gamble with lousy odds. But the heart wanted what it wanted. His heart wanted to spend more time with Rowan.

When he saw her at the campfire, cooking a very large, unwieldy s'more, he walked straight over to her, just when she was trying to open her mouth wide enough to navigate the s'more into her mouth. It was not a successful attempt. The melted, gooey marshmallow was on her face, in her hair, on her hands…

When she noticed him, she waved, completely undeterred by the mess. Her perseverance paid off, and she managed to get what was left of the s'more into her mouth. Chewing triumphantly, she turned up her closed lips into a satisfied smile.

Darn it if his first thought wasn't about kissing that marshmallow right off her lips.

"Hey, Axel!" Rowan waved him over.

"Hey." He liked how she said his name. Silky with a nice dose of flirtation.

"Are you joining us?"

He hadn't considered what would happen once he

reached her. All he knew was he had a primal urge to be by her side. "I guess I could."

"Hey, Axel." Nash stood up and offered his hand to the cowboy.

Mercy greeted him, as well.

"There's room here," Nash said.

Mercy frowned quickly, but Axel saw it and tucked it in the back of his mind. "I don't want to put you folks out."

"You're not!" Nash said. Then to Mercy, he said, "Just scooch down a bit."

"There isn't enough room," the woman argued.

"There is," Nash assured her.

The frown politely wiped away, Rowan's friend smiled and moved down enough for Axel to sit down next to Rowan.

"I'm a mess!" Rowan said with a laugh.

"I see that."

She smiled at him and leaned over and bumped her shoulder to his. "Nice to see you, cowboy."

"Nice to be seen."

"Would you like me to make you one?"

He returned her smile. "I think I'll pass."

"Chicken," Rowan said playfully.

"Good choice, Axel," Nash commented. "We ate margaritas for lunch and dinner."

Loudly, Rowan leaned over to Axel and said, "He's trying to tell you that I'm tipsy."

"I don't think it's a secret." He laughed, loving how clear and blue her eyes were. "Look. I'm off at noon tomorrow. It's going to be a scorcher. Would you like to ride out to the lake? Cool off?"

Rowan bobbed her head. "Yep."

Mercy leaned forward and said in a tone that held some negative emotion, "You can't just keep taking Rowan away from us. We're here to heal. All of us."

"More's the merrier," he said to the group. "Let's all go."

Chapter Four

Rowan realized that drinking wasn't her friend. Drowning her sorrows over Dutton wasn't helping. It was hurting, and not just thanks to the nagging migraine she had. No. She was stronger than this.

"Wait!" Ray Brand, her newly discovered cousin, came running out of the main house carrying a basket. "Here!"

Nash hadn't mounted his horse yet, so he met her halfway.

"You can't have a swim at our lake without a picnic," Ray called out to the party.

"Thank you so much," Rowan said sincerely. The Big Sky Brands had embraced her as one of their own immediately and without a moment's hesitation.

Nash hooked the basket onto the back of his saddle. The basket was resting on the horse's round rump, but not at all in a way that hurt the horse.

Ray walked over to Rowan, her auburn ponytail bouncing with every step. "I fell in love with Dean at the lake."

Rowan laughed self-consciously, her eyes flittering quickly to Axel. "I don't think I'm quite ready to fall in love."

Ray stared at her with the same-colored blue eyes that looked back at her in the mirror. After a moment of awkward silence, Ray patted her horse on the neck and said, "Have a great time!"

Everyone was mounted and now armed with food and drink for this rather impromptu trip. The lake shared property on both Hideaway land and Legend land, an adjacent cattle ranch owned and operated by Ray's first love and now fiancé, Dean. There was a section on the Hideaway Ranch website dedicated to the lake. And, of course, the lake was featured as one of the first examples of the power of the ranch for inspiring love.

It was forecasted to be a sunny day; the weather was on their side. Axel took the lead of their four-person party, while Rowan brought up the rear.

She was certain that there wasn't a child born in Wyoming who hadn't been put on top of a horse before they could walk. Mercy had been one of those kids who sincerely hated to ride horses. So it was rather surprising to Rowan that she had wanted to come on this trip. In her gut, she believed that something was brewing underneath the surface with Mercy. It couldn't be easy, with her high school sweetheart and fiancé being best friends with Dutton.

As they wound their way through the canopy of trees, Rowan began to brace herself for the fallout of her breakup with Dutton that was almost certainly on the horizon. Was her and Mercy's friendship strong enough to withstand this catastrophic event? It pained Rowan to think that there was a small chance, a sliver really, that it couldn't.

Wanting to leave Dutton behind, she trained her eyes on Axel, a handsome cowboy who sat that horse like a pro. Axel represented fun and adventure, and a quick romance with him seemed like exactly what the doctor had ordered. Lord, he was handsome!

Axel whistled as he rode into a clearing. He halted, and the rest of the party came to a stop beside him. A large herd of pronghorn antelope had stopped at the lake to drink. When he whistled, the herd lifted up their heads in unison and looked at them. Then they turned tail and ran as fast as they could across the large field and into the woods on the other side of the lake.

"Okay," Mercy said, "this is God showing off."

That made Rowan laugh. "My thoughts exactly."

There was a magic surrounding this lake. It was pristine, a spring-fed lake with Montana wild flowers adding splashes of vibrant color. There was an old dock that looked rather rickety, and some spots on the grass that seemed perfect for a picnic.

Rowan snapped off some pictures to post and then she rode in a line with her friends and resident hot cowboy to the lake with a history of making love matches. Once she dismounted, she let her horse graze nearby with the other four, all experienced quarter horses who had been taught to ground tie since they were foals.

Mercy spread out her towel, sat down and, in a floppy, bright pink hat and large sunglasses that nearly engulfed her face, began to apply sun lotion.

"Aren't you going to swim?" Rowan asked, pulling off her T-shirt and slipping out of her jeans.

"No." Mercy shook her head. "I'll be fine here."

Rowan paused, weighing the idea of pursuing the reason behind the frown on Mercy's face. But then she was distracted by Axel taking off his jeans, standing on the end of the dock, the soft sunlight casting a warm yellow glow to his tanned, sculpted body. The abs, the biceps, the thighs…

"That man isn't a snack," Rowan said out loud. "He's the whole meal."

"He certainly seems to like you." Mercy frowned even deeper. It made Rowan shake her head in frustration. Would her ex-fiancé manage to ruin her attempt to move on from his betrayal? She already cried for him at night. She already felt the absence of him in her life and that didn't stop just because he'd cheated on her and produced a child. It was complicated and convoluted, and nothing made sense. She missed him. She missed their talks. He was an interesting man. He was handsome. He had always been able to make her laugh and not take life so seriously. Now he was gone.

Axel dove into the lake, disappeared, and then shot back out of the water, which glistened on his shoulders and chest. He slicked his blond hair off his handsome face, and Rowan felt her knees buckle. Just a little.

He looked over at her and waved. "Come on in!"

Nash had stripped down to his bathing trunks and jumped in, as well. He called out to Mercy; he had always been focused on Mercy. "Come on, Mercy!" Nash waved at her. "It's the perfect temperature."

"No!" She shook her head. "I'm fine here."

When Rowan focused on Axel, her mind got a reprieve from mulling over all things Dutton. And she was going to darn well take advantage of it. She picked her way over to the dock, the jagged rocks making her wince occasionally. Once on the dock, with all of Axel's attention on her, she felt self-conscious. The man looked at her like he wanted to devour her. In all her time with Dutton, he had never once looked at her like that.

"Watch this," Nash told Axel, gesturing at Rowan.

Glad she had worn a one-piece bathing suit, Rowan stood at the end of the dock, turned her back toward the lake, closed her eyes, concentrated, and then she pushed off and dived backward into the lake.

When she reemerged, she was laughing, pushing her wild hair off her face along with the water. She bobbed in the lake, so cool instead of cold.

"Where did you learn to do that?" Axel asked, seeming truly impressed.

"Fit camp." She shared a look with Nash.

"What the heck is that?" Axel asked.

"Fat camp," Rowan clarified, not ashamed anymore. As a kid, she'd been overweight, and her parents had sent her to a camp to help her get fit, not just lose weight. That was where she had met Nash, and that was the reason she was and would always be tied to Nash in a way that transcended just mere friendship.

Axel didn't seem the least bit fazed. "Well, it worked."

Nash and she shared a laugh, and then Axel asked her, "What else do you got?"

"Is that some sort of challenge?" she asked him playfully.

"Maybe." He winked at her with a grin as he swam closer.

The butterflies were there. The excitement of attraction was there. So unexpected, but she was grateful for it. "What can you do?" Rowan asked him.

"Cannonball."

"Are you serious?" Rowan asked. "The cannonball."

"Zero skill." Nash joined in. "Rowan won the blue ribbon for diving at fit camp. That's no joke, man."

"Do you know what, Axel? I'm going to meet you where you're at. Whoever makes the biggest splash gets to pick the next date."

"You're on."

Out of the corner of her eye, she saw Mercy bow her head down. She didn't want to hurt her friend. Ever. But it was just reality that their "Dutton, Douglas, Mercy, and Rowan" quartet was irreparably broken. And, right now, she was in self-preservation mode, grasping at anything that could reduce her pain, her sense of loss. The pain of losing Dutton wasn't only emotional or mental. She felt it like a pain in her body—overworked tear ducts, aching in her joints and her muscles. Her stomach was upset all hours of the day.

She swam to the edge of the lake. Nash got out and sat down on a towel next to Mercy.

"Can you take a video?" Rowan asked Nash.

"Absolutely." He held up his phone.

Axel got out of the water and watched her from the

bank. Poised on the first board of the dock, Rowan looked at Nash for his signal.

"I'm rolling," he told her. "Ready. Get set. Go!"

Rowan always gave it her all. She was competitive. Always had been. She sprinted down the dock and launched herself forward, curled her legs beneath her body and dropped into the water with what she assumed was a winning splash.

She resurfaced. "Well?"

Nash gave her a thumbs-up. "Got it!"

Then it was Axel's turn. Rowan booed from the edge of the lake.

"She's a sore loser," Nash said.

"That's okay," Axel said confidently. "She can make it up to me on our second date."

Axel appeared to be as competitive as Rowan was, and she liked that about him. He ignored her catcalls as he ran down the dock, hurled himself into the air and then dropped into the water. The splash was so big that more than a few droplets landed on her face.

"Darn it!" she said loudly. "Let me see the replay."

Axel came out of the water and joined them while Nash replayed the video.

"That felt good." The cowboy smiled at her.

"You won," Nash said to Axel. "Hands down."

Mercy, who had been quiet for most of the time at the lake, said, "That's hardly fair. Axel weighs more."

"Good point, Mercy." Rowan nodded. "That's unfair."

"I'll forfeit, if that's what you want," Axel said, his

arms crossed casually in front of his body, a glint in his eye that was oh so magnetic.

"No." Rowan shook her head, eyebrows drawn together. "I don't want or need your pity. Where are we going for date number two?"

Axel felt odd. Uncomfortable in his own skin, but he knew how to keep those feelings under wraps. Rowan Brand did something to him that made him want to turn and hightail it to the hills. He'd experienced this feeling once or twice before. It always came out of the blue and, in the end, tended to leave him brokenhearted. But he couldn't stop looking at Rowan. He admired her fun-loving personality, just as he admired her face that was meant for the admiration of others.

He told Rowan he'd get back with her about date number two, and they all sat down on their blankets to eat the lunch Ray had prepared for them.

"The woman is obviously a genius in the kitchen," Nash said, finishing off his second sandwich. He chased it with sun-brewed iced tea sweetened with local honeysuckle honey.

"Amen," Axel agreed.

Rowan had chosen to sit next to him, their bodies touching now and again. He felt Mercy's eyes on him, and even though she tried to hide it, there was a world of hurt behind her guarded eyes. He didn't take it personally. From what he understood, Mercy had been caught up in the breakup of Rowan and her ex.

"I think I need to head back," Mercy said, standing up.

"Why leave so soon?" Rowan asked her.

Mercy folded her towel, cleaned up her area and said, "I have a migraine."

"I'm sorry," Rowan said sympathetically.

Nash stood up. "I'll head back with you."

Mercy nodded. Rowan stood up and hugged her friend tightly. "I hope you feel better. I'll check on you when I get back."

"No hurry," Mercy said. "You deserve to enjoy your time."

Nash and Mercy mounted and then disappeared into the woods on a brightly marked trail that led back to the center of the ranch.

Rowan sat down, tilted her head back and let the sun warm her face. She was just so darned pretty.

"Mercy hasn't taken a shine to me," Axel said.

Rowan breathed in and let it out slowly before she lowered her chin and opened her eyes. "It's not you."

"No," he agreed. "I figured that much."

Sitting cross-legged, Rowan said, "We don't have a road map for this. What do we do when we've been a foursome for a long time, and now that foursome has imploded?"

"Gotta be tough."

Rowan nodded. "We're both mourning a loss here."

Axel wasn't sure what to say, so he kept his powder dry.

"She's in a horrible position. Her fiancé is Dutton's best friend. It's a mess."

Axel realized that he had led Rowan down a path

unintended. Rowan seemed to smile whenever he was around, and he'd like to keep it going that way.

The first thing that came to mind was a quick kiss on her flushed cheeks. He leaned over and kissed her quick. She reacted exactly as he had hoped: with a surprised but happy smile. He stood up and ran toward the dock, and she chased him. His spitfire.

At the end of the dock, he waited for her to catch him. She tried to push him in, but he had already made a plan to handle that eventuality. He leaned down, scooped her up, and while she demanded that he put her down, he laughed and jumped in with her in his arms.

They both came up to the surface, coughing and plugging their noses.

"Axel!"

"Present and accounted for," he said, shaking his head and trying to get the water out of his ears.

"The object of swimming is to *not* drown."

"Note taken." He laughed.

She was laughing, too, and he was happy to see her smile. He surely did like her smile. Unexpectedly and totally welcome, Rowan swam over to him and hooked her arms around his neck.

"You're a good time, cowboy," she said. "Dancing, horseback riding, swimming. What else do you have up your sleeve?"

The moment was presented to him, and he took it. He leaned his head down, giving the pretty cowgirl all of the chance in the world to stop it, and she didn't. Their lips touched, light, dewy, sweet. For him, a kiss like no other.

"What was that about?"

He smiled. "You wanted me to kiss you, so I complied."

She pushed away from him and splashed water at him.

"Don't pick a fight if you don't want to tussle," he told her.

"I'll tussle with you any time you want."

"You might just regret that you said that." He swam to catch up with her. She climbed out onto the bank, laughing, just as pretty as a young lady could be. He climbed out after her, and when he went for a second kiss, she grabbed his arm, pulled him off balance and then pushed him into the water.

He was genuinely shocked. He'd never been knocked over by a woman who couldn't be more than one hundred and forty pounds. But damn it, she had.

Rowan gave him a sassy smile, and she looked mighty fine in that swimsuit coming and going. At the picnic area, she took off his hat that he'd put on a stick in the ground as a makeshift hat rack. Rowan looked over her shoulder at him, flirty, then put on his hat.

"Rowan?"

"Yes, Axel?"

"Don't mess with a man's hat. That's just good manners."

"How do I look in your hat?"

"Like it was made for you."

He wanted to be with Rowan in the worst way. He liked her. He sure as heck was attracted to her. But no doubt about it, Rowan was looking for a good time, not a lifetime. Perhaps the flirting had gone too far.

His pretty redhead had an odd expression on her face as she put his hat back on the stick. "We'd better get back," she said, drying off her body before she put on her jeans, T-shirt and boots.

"Sure," he said, doing the same.

They packed up quick and then both mounted.

"I hope you had a good time," he said, riding next to her when the trail would allow.

"I've had the best time," she said without hesitation. "Just what I needed."

That made him feel good on the inside, yet he sensed something that made him want to give her an out. She had suffered a horrible breakup. She didn't need him creeping up on her if she didn't really want it.

"You can get out of the date," he said at last.

Rowan's head swiveled around quickly, and she had a quizzical expression on her face. "What makes you think I want out?"

"Just giving you one, is all."

"Hey. If you're trying to get out of it, no problem."

He halted his horse. "Whoa. Wait a minute."

She did.

"I'm not trying to get out of our date," he said. "Let's get that straight."

"Okay. I don't want an out, either."

"Okay."

"All righty then."

"Fine."

"Exactly."

Their banter lightened the mood, and they continued on the path, laughing. It was so easy with Rowan. It just was.

"Is there a wish list of things you'd like to do?"

"No." She shrugged. "Just make sure base jumping and sky diving aren't on it."

"Good to know."

They finished the way back in silence. When they dismounted, Rowan thanked him.

"I'm glad you enjoyed it."

"I did." She reached out and put her hand on his arm. "Thank you."

They said goodbye, and he took care of the horses and then carried the picnic basket into the main house.

Ray wasn't there, but Danny was. The triplets were a handful, that was just the truth. Ray was sweet, kind and creative, always thinking of others. Charlie was a cowgirl rancher to the core of her being. And Danny? Tough-as-nails businesswoman.

"Did you have a good time?" Danny asked.

"I did."

"And the guests?"

"All good."

Danny took her reading glasses off and pinned him on the spot with her sharp blue eyes, so similar to Rowan's. "Anything to report?"

Axel knew what she was angling at. Danny's waking moments, and probably even her dreams, were focused on branding the ranch as the place where love always bloomed and was always in season.

"No." He shook his head, praying that a lightning bolt didn't strike him dead for lying to one of his bosses. That kiss he shared with Rowan had been special, and he hadn't had a real chance to digest it, think about it, figure it out.

"Well." Danny put her glasses back on and refocused on her computer. "I expect a report if anything changes."

"Yes, ma'am." Axel tipped his brim as he headed to the door. "I surely will. You'll be the very first to know."

Chapter Five

Nash Landry had spent an hour with Mercy, scrolling through her social media accounts and helping select pictures she should post. They discussed lighting, clothing choices and makeup. It felt lame to him, this ritual that they had, but he had always taken any and every opportunity to spend time with Mercy.

For him, it was a painful, unrequited love. What had started as a crush when they were kids had turned into a full-blown, one-sided love affair. Along the way, he had casually dated some very lovely girls, perfect girls for him, really, yet none of them stuck. In his mind, he just couldn't move past Mercy.

When she got engaged to Douglas, with his buff body and tried and true rancher bio, it had felt like his heart refused to beat the way it had before. But even now, knowing she was engaged, knowing she was picking out her wedding dresses because she had asked him to go on all of her dress hunting trips, Nash couldn't dislodge Mercy from his head or his heart.

"Oh!" Mercy exclaimed, her eyes shining brightly at her phone. "It's my hubby."

Nash stood up and left the room, his head down,

shaking it with anger toward himself. Every time Mercy called Doug her "hubby," it cut him up on the inside. He pushed his brown hair off his forehead and walked right into a wall. "Damn. Who put that there?"

"Oh, Nash," Rowan said. She had been resting on the couch. She sat up, took one look at him, and met him where he was standing. She didn't have to ask, and he didn't have to say it. She hugged him tightly.

"Nash," she said. "You have to stop. You can't keep being Mercy's purse holder and stylist."

"I know," he agreed quietly. "I know. I just can't stand the fact that she's going to marry a guy who calls himself D. Dog."

"But she *is* going to marry him. You have to accept it. As do I." Rowan stepped back and met his gaze. "This is it, my dear friend. This is the time; this is the place. When we leave here, we will leave the old baggage behind and start anew. You are so handsome, you have so much to give a woman, and you need to find a woman who appreciates you."

"I don't see myself like that," he admitted to her.

"I know you don't. I've struggled with my image, too. But would I lie to you?"

"No. You'd just find something else to compliment me about."

She nodded. "Bingo."

He knew she was right. Of course, she was right. Sometimes in his own indulgence in self-pity, he forgot to check in with the people he loved. "How are you coping?" he asked.

Rowan sighed, and there was a flicker of sadness

and pain. It was fleeting because Rowan was tough. Hardened by the Wyoming way of life. "I'm coping," she said simply.

"Axel is a fun diversion."

"He is." Rowan nodded. "You need your own."

He couldn't deny it. They hugged again. Tightly.

"You are such a handsome man, Nash. Kind, brilliant, caring. If you want to find your person, and she is out there, you have to let go of the impossible."

He ducked his head. When he looked in the mirror, he still saw the chunky boy he once was. Yes, dinosaur hunting, something he was innately skilled at, had raised his profile with his family, especially his father, and that had given him a much-needed boost of confidence. But it was still difficult to move past that image of himself when he was an odd, obese kid.

"Better?" she asked him.

He nodded. "Better."

"Good." Rowan smiled as she turned his body toward the door, giving him a friendly push. "Now go forth and find your destiny!"

"What are you going to do?"

"My destiny is to lie back down on that couch."

Just as they finished their conversation and Rowan was heading back to the couch and he to the front door, Mercy opened the door to her room, a sparkle in her eye and a broad smile on her face.

"Nash! Are you coming back? There are still a ton of pictures to sort."

Almost every fiber in his being wanted to head back to her room, just to be near her, record moments with her, but Rowan's talk had been more transformative than he might have guessed. There was one fiber, the loudest as it turned out, that was shouting in his brain—*move on!*

"Maybe later," he said.

Mercy's lovely round face registered both surprise and disappointment. This was, he realized, the first time he had *not* accepted an invitation from her.

And it feels good.

He waved at her and caught Rowan's eye as he headed out the door. He rolled his shoulders back, raised his chin, took his cowboy hat off the rack and put it on, brim slightly down to hood his eyes. Then he headed out of the door.

He closed his eyes and took in a deep breath. Rowan had called it. This was the moment to start over. He opened his eyes and walked forward to wherever his new cowboy boots were going to take him.

Rowan had taken a long nap on the couch and awakened with food on her brain.

Mercy had some serious Spidey senses when it came to food. She opened her door and intercepted her on the way to the kitchen. "I'm famished," she said, her hair pulled up into one high ponytail.

"Me, too," Rowan agreed. "I think I'm definitely eating my emotions."

"Same."

Together, they foraged through the kitchen, scanning the fridge and the pantry.

"Cheese plate?" Mercy asked. "Hummus?"

"Heck yeah."

They carried the food to the table, poured some sweet tea into heavy pottery mugs and then sat down at the table together. Rowan tore through the cheddar cheese cubes and then scooped up the hummus with hunks of Italian bread.

"Mmm," Mercy said.

"OMG, yes."

Rowan topped off her friend's glass with sweet tea and then refilled her own. She downed another whole glass and finally felt satisfied.

"Where did Nash go?" Mercy asked, taking small nibbles of bread and hummus. She was always very conscientious of her figure, and Rowan knew all too well that Doug put pressure on Mercy to keep her weight consistent. It bothered her, but Mercy was just as stuck on Doug as Rowan had been with Dutton. Those blinders were real and almost impossible to remove from the outside looking in.

"Not sure," Rowan said, dipping a cracker into the hummus. "Just out, I suppose."

Mercy furrowed her brows. "Was he acting weird? I think he was acting weird."

Rowan let out a loud breath, brushed her hands together to dislodge any crumbs and then wiped her face with a napkin.

"He's never said no to helping me out," Mercy said, and Rowan could see that she was legitimately hurt. Of course, Mercy loved Nash. But as a friend. Not *ever* as a suitor.

"I talked to him."

This brief talk with Nash hadn't been the first. Cassady always tried to talk sense into him and so had Rowan. This time, Rowan felt that she might have somehow broken what had always been an impenetrable wall in Nash's head.

Mercy stopped eating and focused all her attention on her.

"I told him it was time to break things off with you."

Mercy shook her head several times as if shaking the water off her face after a swim. "Break things off?" Her volume rose a notch. "What did you mean by that?"

Rowan took in a deep breath of her own and then looked her friend straight in the eye. "Nash has been in love with you for years, Mercy. You know that."

Mercy frowned and crossed her arms. "No, I do not know that."

"Yes, you do know," Rowan said firmly. "It's the elephant in every blessed room, at every blessed event!"

Mercy lowered her head, shaking it.

"Mercy. This Band-Aid had to be ripped off. You're less than a year away from marrying Doug. It's not fair to have Nash trailing behind you like a faithful puppy, hoping one day you will return his abiding love for you."

Her friend was quiet now. Unusually so.

"This isn't the first time you're hearing this," Rowan said softly. Mercy was close to tears.

"No," Mercy said. "It isn't. Cassady always verbally bashes me over the head about it. She thinks I'm so trite and pathetic anyway."

"No, she doesn't. She loves you. Her delivery is too harsh. But the message isn't wrong."

Mercy looked at her. "You guys act as if I don't love him. But I do love him."

"Yes. As a friend," Rowan reiterated. "Not as a husband."

"Well, no. I have Douglas."

"Then let him go," Rowan encouraged. "Let him get on with it. Once you marry Doug, Nash will be lost without you, and that's not fair. Best to do it now. Let him hurt, heal and let his heart find someone of his own. Someone who will love him as much as he loves them."

Her friend dropped her face into hands and started to cry.

Rowan was at her side, her arms around her. "It's just not fair, Mercy."

Mercy nodded, lifted her head and rubbed the tears from her eyes with a nearby napkin. "I'll let him go."

"He isn't dying, Mercy." Rowan laughed softly. "You'll always have a dear friend."

Mercy nodded again, wiping away more tears.

Rowan gave her another hug. Their friend group, once so strong and seemingly unbreakable, was showing deep cracks as of late. Was her broken engagement with Dutton a trend versus a single anomaly?

Cassady had bolted out of Wyoming the first opportunity and rarely returned to visit her family. She wasn't ranch-life material, and her wild fashion sense that had more masculine notes than feminine staples had been an embarrassment to her ultra-conservative family. Her *I don't give a damn* attitude only deepened the divide between her and her kin.

Mercy was engaged to a man whose best friend had just broken his engagement in an objectively horrible way.

And now, Nash had to distance himself from Mercy for his own self-preservation. Would that fissure grow into a cavern too wide to cross?

Mercy patted her arm, and Rowan stopped hugging her. Yes, Mercy was the most outwardly emotional of their foursome, but she was tougher than she looked. On the outside she was as sweet and fluffy and girly as cotton candy, but under all of those frills and bows, Mercy had a spine of steel.

"It's okay." Mercy straightened her shoulders and lifted her chin. "I'm okay."

Rowan backed off. Her role had been played out.

They cleared the table, washed the dishes, and then Mercy said, "It's the changes that hit me the hardest."

Rowan understood. It was all happening so fast, like a volcano erupting. They had all lived in its shadow, knowing that there was something bubbling up but never really believing that it would erupt. And then it had.

"We'll always be friends," Mercy said.

"Yes," Rowan agreed. "We will."

Yet, she wondered just how they could remain close when Mercy's life was joined with Doug's life. When Doug's best friend, Rowan's ex-fiancé, was at every event. No one was really saying it, not even Cassady, but they all had to be thinking it.

In the blink of an eye, everything could change. Perhaps the events at her rehearsal dinner had been that blink of an eye.

Axel had Rowan on the brain. While he worked, while he relaxed, and when he drifted off to sleep. *Rowan.* Man, she was something else. It wasn't just about looks—even though she had that covered—it was about her humor, her tenacity and her love of just having a good time.

It had been quite a while since a woman had really caught his eye. There were and had always been women in his life. And those that he had loved were still in his heart. When he hit the milestone of his thirtieth birthday, he started to think about settling down, maybe get that house with a white picket fence and have a couple of kids. His lifestyle didn't give him much of a chance to settle, but he would. For the right woman, of course he would.

"Can you turn on that switch over yonder?" Cody Ty Hawkins asked him.

Axel had been on pasture duty with Wayne Westbrook and living legend Cody. One of the best rodeo riders in the history of the sport, Cody had taken a job at Hideaway Ranch.

Charlie wanted several automatic waterers in the new pasture built specifically for the miniature cows that were arriving in the near future. With a backhoe and some ingenuity, they had dug several trenches above the freeze barrier and hooked them to the recently dug well. The well pump needed electricity, as did the waterers, so in the weeks prior they had worked with a local electrician to wire everything up to solar panels.

Now was the moment of truth. Had they done everything right to get water to the cattle once they arrived?

Axel flipped the switch, waited a second or two, and then he heard Wayne give a whoop.

Cody gave him a thumbs-up, and Axel felt pride in the work they had done. He'd been a part of so many ranches, ever since he was a kid, really. Hideaway was the very best. If he had his way, and if his heart didn't take him away from Montana, he'd stay with the Brand sisters for as long as they would have him. It just felt like home.

"It's fresh and cold," Cody said, scooping up some of the water flowing into the reservoir and cooling off the back of his neck.

Wayne sent a message to his fiancé, Charlie, to come inspect the progress. Axel looked at the two older men. They were the type of men he strove to be: solid, rugged and lots of learning from the school of hard knocks. Cowboys who had spent too much time on the road, but managed to find love right here on Hideaway Ranch, Wayne with Charlie, and Cody with a budding romance writer, Journey, and her son, Oakley. Perhaps Hideaway magic was already working on him and Rowan.

Charlie galloped toward them fill tilt on a huge black horse. Her silver hair was tied back into a ponytail, one hand holding on to her cowgirl hat.

"Watch this," Wayne said to him.

Charlie was still approaching them at a gallop, as if

she was planning to knock down all three of them like a bowling ball hitting the pins.

Axel backed up, but Wayne stopped him.

Wayne's wild-spirited cowgirl leaned back a bit, and the horse slid to a halt. Charlie took her feet out of the stirrups, swung her leg over the horse's neck, and hopped down to the ground.

"Damn," Axel muttered.

"Damn is right," Wayne agreed, before he kissed his soon-to-be bride.

Charlie strode away from her fiancé to examine the waterer. "This looks pretty good."

"Don't hurt yourself with effusive praise," Wayne said with a playful tone in his voice. "None of us men need it."

"I don't need it," Cody said.

"Me, neither." Axel stood his ground, arms crossed.

That made Charlie crack a smile as she hugged Wayne. "Okay. This is great! Amazing! I've never been so impressed."

They all had a good laugh before Charlie, as was her personality, asked, "So, three more to go? Will they be done by end of day?"

Cody and Wayne smiled at each other. "Most likely."

Charlie shook her head with a frown. "I need you to turn that most likely into a most definitely."

Wayne put his arm around her and hugged her to him. "Who thought it was a good idea to get into the miniature cow business?"

"Do not even get me started," Charlie said. Then she looked right at Axel, and it made him feel like he was about to get scolded by the nuns from the Catholic school he'd attended. "Wayne told me to let Ray be Ray."

"I don't remember it quite that way," Wayne commented.

Charlie said to Axel, "Don't let him poison your mind. He said it, and I did it, and now Ray has got us into the pet miniature cow business, along with her miniature donkeys, fainting goats and chickens."

Wayne cracked a sheepish smile. "I'm beginning to wonder if that was the best advice."

"Ya think?" Charlie asked, kidding, before she swung back into her saddle. She gave them a quick wave, spun her horse around and galloped away.

"That's quite a woman you have there," Cody said.

"That's the God honest truth," Wayne agreed.

"We're both lucky," Cody said to his friend. "Good women totally out of our league."

There was a question in Axel's mind. It'd been rolling around like a wash cycle until it was spinning so fast it was impossible to ignore. So, he asked.

"Just for conversation purposes," he said to the older cowboys. "How did you know?"

"Know what?" Wayne asked.

"That she was the one."

That made both Cody and Wayne crack a smile. Then, Wayne said, "It was like being run over by a freight train. It wasn't subtle."

Cody nodded. "Sucker punch to the gut. Nearly bent me in half, it hurt so bad."

And that was that. They weren't offering more, and

Axel didn't need to belabor the subject. If he needed more information, he could ask later. For now, they had a job to do here. That had to be his focus.

As they covered the water pipe with dirt so they could start digging the next trench, Axel thought about the good women in Wayne and Cody's lives. He wanted a good woman in his life. In Rowan, he was pretty sure he'd found one. It hadn't felt exactly like a sucker punch to the heart or being run over by a freight train. He liked her. She was fun loving, adventurous, strong and had a great sense of humor. But she was brokenhearted. Would she ever give him a true shot at winning her heart, or would she take him for a good time and then head on back to her life?

"Get your mind back in the game, son," Cody said to him.

Cody's words snapped him back to the present. The elder cowboy was right. It was easy for a man to get hurt on a ranch. He'd been plenty banged up—broken arm and wrist, back bent all out of shape, concussions, and almost lost his ring finger on his right hand. More scratches, rashes, bruises and burns than he could remember.

Axel jogged over to the backhoe to dig where Wayne was directing. He had to refocus his mind frequently, because his brain just kept on circling back to Rowan.

He wanted to treat her real nice, take her out for a nice dinner. Maybe some wine. He'd gotten paid. Nice, fat check. As soon as Wayne said he could knock off for the day, he was going to clean himself up, so he didn't smell like a giant cow patty, then head to her door, a bouquet of wild flowers in his hand. How could the pretty Wyoming girl say no?

"Maybe she could," Axel said as he headed back to the bunkhouse. "But I sure as heck hope she doesn't."

Once he reached the bunkhouse, he shot a text to Rowan with the invitation and then waited impatiently for her to respond. And then she did.

"Yes!" Axel celebrated. Time to find some decent clothes to wear. This might require a quick trip to town. He needed to dress to impress.

Chapter Six

"What do you think?" Rowan asked, spinning around so the skirt of her minidress would swing out around her, showing off her shapely alabaster legs to their best effect.

Mercy, who was lying on her bed, gave two thumbs up. "It's perfect. You're perfect. Dutton would love you in this."

Rowan stopped twirling.

Mercy slapped her hand over her mouth. "I am so sorry. Why am I having a harder time with all of this than you?"

"Because you feel everything so deeply, Mercy. It's a blessing and a curse." Rowan sat down next to her friend, put her arms around her shoulders and gave her a reassuring hug. "I am struggling with all of this, too. I just like to hide it in dark, murky water overrun with slippery, nasty, stinky red algae."

"Gosh." Mercy grimaced. "That's terrible."

And they both laughed, which helped lighten the mood. They didn't have a playbook for the mess Dutton had created with his betrayal. They would just have to learn as they went.

"We promised each other that everything between us would stay the same," Mercy said.

"Of course."

"But it's already changing." Mercy pinched the sides of her nose to stop the tears from falling. "You're already dating!"

That made Rowan laugh. "It's a shock to me as well, trust me. But a sexy cowboy landing in my life, like a gift from heaven above, is fixing some of what ails me, Mercy. At least I'm not sitting around pining for Dutton."

"Well, would it hurt for you to pine some? I thought for sure we would be binge watching something on Netflix, eating our feelings with popcorn and ice cream."

"I promise," Rowan said. "Tomorrow, we pine!"

It had felt weird to say Dutton's name. She had thought it a hundred times, but it hadn't crossed her lips.

"Douglas told me you blocked Dutton."

"Of course I did. Self-preservation."

"I know." Mercy stood up, walked over to the nearby vanity and patted the chair with her hand. "It's just one more domino."

Rowan moved to the chair. "I think there will be just one more domino for a while."

Mercy nodded. "Well. Let's change the subject to something much more important." Mercy stood behind her, brush in hand. "I know just what to do with your makeup. How do you want to wear your hair?"

Axel checked himself out in the bathroom mirror. He wasn't one to worry about his appearance, until recently. There was something unique about his feelings for Rowan, and that unique something made him want to impress her.

Everything was new. Because the clientele at Big Sky Resort were mainly crazy wealthy and a studio apartment carried a price tag of one million dollars, finding a shop with an upscale Western style was easy. The salesman fit him with dark-wash jeans, a tucked-in button-down blue-and-white shirt and a sport coat to finish the look. He already had boots and a hat for the rare special occasion. He brushed his longish blond hair back off his face. He'd almost gotten a cut, but in the end, he'd thought against it. That would look like he was trying too hard.

And even though he *was* trying hard, he didn't want to clue Rowan in. He needed to play it cool.

"She'll approve." Nash was lying on his back in the top bunk he had claimed, reading a book.

Axel tugged on either side of the jacket, rolling his neck a bit, trying to feel comfortable. "Too much?" he asked. Nash knew Rowan.

Nash put his book down and sat up. "With Rowan, it's never too much. Grand gestures are always appreciated. Being decked out for a date? Put a one in your score column."

"Thanks. I appreciate you, Nash." Axel took his best Stetson out of his locker and put it on. "I'll see you later, brother."

"I'll see you tomorrow at sunrise if Rowan is having a good time."

That made Axel laugh and made him feel less stiff

in his getup. He walked over to his truck that had been cleaned inside and out, then drove to the cabin to pick Rowan up.

At the door, he felt his pulse quicken, his face flush, his palms go clammy.

God bless. Where was the cooler-than-a-cucumber-in-a-deep-freezer attitude? Was that the freight train deal Wayne had been talking about? But Axel didn't feel like he'd been punched in the face or anywhere else on his body. And that was a good thing, because Rowan was a bad bet.

Now, that didn't stop him from taking a gamble on her. But the truth had to be acknowledged.

"Hi!" Rowan swung open the door, wearing a blue denim minidress. Nothing too revealing but sexy as all get-out. She was wearing her thick auburn hair clipped back from her face with the rest curled into spirals that bounced when she moved her head.

"You look incredible," he said. All of his pseudo-coolness drained out of his brain the minute she opened the door. Flawless makeup, twinkling sapphire blue eyes… Man, she was a knockout and darn it! He did feel like he just got sucker punched in the gut, just as Cody Ty had described!

"Thank you," she said, walking through the door. "You look incredible, too."

"I try."

"You clearly succeed."

Over his date's shoulder, Mercy yelled, "Curfew is ten o'clock, you two!"

Rowan kept smiling at him as she shut the door. “Not a chance.”

“Music to my ears.” Axel offered her his arm, which she took.

“Pulling out all of the stops,” Rowan noted. “I like it.”

“Higher the truck, the closer to God,” Rowan said, putting on her seat belt.

“Do you want to get hitched?” he teased back and then realized what he had just said. “Damn, Rowan. I’m sorry. That was a real jackass thing to say.”

“No!” she said. “Don’t you take it back. It’s easier if we make light of it. It would hurt too much if we didn’t.”

Still not convinced, Axel shut the passenger door and walked around to the driver’s side.

When he got behind the wheel, Rowan reached out her hand and put it on his arm. “I’m serious, Axel.” She was clearly doing her best to make him feel better. “I have to laugh about it, or I would spend all of my time at this beautiful ranch crying. I much prefer going out to dinner with a handsome cowboy.”

“Okay.” He cranked the engine. “If you say so.”

“I do.”

And that was his experience with Rowan thus far. She was a woman who, even in her own loss, wanted to make him feel more comfortable.

“You sure are nice, Rowan.”

He glanced over at her, and she smiled prettily at him with a flush on her freckled cheeks. She tucked some curls behind her ear and said, "You sure are nice, too, Axel. Thank you for asking me out for dinner."

"My pleasure."

Rowan had known that Axel was handsome. He was objectively so. In that sport coat and blue shirt that turned his eyes a striking turquoise, she found it rather difficult to stop herself from staring at him. Even the long, faint scar on his jawline only added to his appeal.

What a stroke of luck, meeting him on her first night in Montana. Axel was the exact distraction she needed. Even with her attempt to eradicate Dutton from her online and in-person life, she had received several *you have this person in common with everyone else in your life* nudges from the social platforms to follow Dutton, who now had a picture of himself and his Mensa member girlfriend with those dark features and a smile that lit up her entire face. They were arm in arm, very close and cozy.

There was a part of Rowan in total denial, still searching for the silver lining that would erase this moment and time and put her back into the arms of her beloved. Yet, there he was, all smiles with his baby mama. Moving on with his life as if he hadn't left a steaming pile of garbage in his wake. He seemed blithely unaware of the fact that her mom was frantically trying to cancel the venue, the caterers, the horse-drawn carriage, DJs, florist, bartenders, entertainers, photographers, videographers and the one hundred and fifty mini cakes that mirrored the eight-tiered wedding cake.

The amount of money her parents had spent on giving her the wedding of her childhood dreams was horribly astounding, and most of it was lost. Dutton was quiet on this topic, and his parents had been noticeably absent from their church. It had all felt like a nightmare; she would wake up soon, she was sure.

But seeing Dutton, seemingly happy to have moved on, hit her so hard that she had sat on the edge of her bed, her thoughts plummeting into the lowest part of mind. She'd been in the muck and the dark, and then, miraculously, a text had come from Axel. He had thrown her a lifeline and didn't even know it. Would most likely never know it. After all, Dutton was her past and Axel was her "right now."

"So." She turned her body toward him. "Tell me all about Axel Redford."

He had a lopsided grin, dimples and a sexy wink. Lord help her! "What do you want to know?"

"What do you want me to know?"

They laughed easily together. They clicked, and that allowed Rowan to let down her hair, so to speak, and just enjoy the moment with this handsome rancher.

"My parents met at some point, copulated, and then I came along."

Still laughing, she shook her head. "Let's start later. Were you honor roll or hellion?"

He laughed with her. "You guess."

"Hmm." Rowan tapped her fingertip on her upper lip. "Let me think."

"Don't judge me. Look past the cover. Be open-minded."

"You were on the honor roll?" she asked, her freshly shaped eyebrows lifted in surprise.

"Nope." He shook his head. "Kicked out of Catholic school. Parents very unhappy with me about that."

"I'm sure."

"Then, I was kicked out of public school in the tenth grade for fighting. And possession of a substance that today is widely accepted as medicinal."

She crossed her arms playfully over her chest. "You fooled me."

"No. I misled you," he countered. "But you deserved it. Judging me the way that you did."

She couldn't deny it. She had judged him a smidge. "Okay. I grant you that."

"Kind of you."

"Tell me something else."

"Not much to tell, really," Axel said, and this was the first time in the short time she had known him that she detected an undertone of sadness in his voice. "Grew up in Colorado. I have two sisters. Both older."

"Oh!" she interjected. "The baby of the family. You do give off baby-of-the-family vibes."

"I resemble that remark." He winked at her.

"Are you close with your sisters?"

"Tight." He nodded. "They've started to have kids. They both bought houses in the same neighborhood we grew up in."

"That's amazing," she said sincerely. "Is that what you want?"

He thought about it for a moment or two. "Some days I think so when I'm missing them bad."

"So on those days, same neighborhood, white picket fence? Kids?"

"All of that."

"And on the days you don't want that?"

"Ranchin'. It's in my blood now," he said easily with a glance over at her. "What about you?"

"Me?" she asked with a squeak in her voice. "I've always wanted to be a mom. Yes, a career, but it's so easy to work from home nowadays. I don't need to choose baby or business."

There was a silence between them, and it was difficult for Rowan to process what had just been shared with her. It was deep and emotional. She felt rather honored he would let her in so quickly, but it also made her feel skittish.

Axel was supposed to be her post-breakup fling that would reset her brain and help her find a new path forward in Wyoming. She had no plans to live anywhere else. Dutton was the creep! If anyone should scurry away, it should be him!

"Did I lose you?" Axel broke the silence.

"No!" she was quick to say. "I'm sorry. Sometimes I get into my own head."

They managed to get themselves back to lighthearted, singing off-key to all the country songs that came on the radio. Next thing, they pulled up to a restaurant, Michelangelo's.

"I hope you like Italian." Axel pulled into a parking space and cut the engine. "I guess I should have asked."

"I L. O. V. E. Italian."

"Glad to hear it." Axel jumped out, rounded the hood of his truck and met her on the other side.

When she put her hand in his, she felt something pulsing in her body. It was different, unusual and, with the current available data, completely inexplicable. It had to be chemistry, falling into lust, perhaps? With Dutton, it had always just been there. Not super exciting but familiar. Safe.

"I don't need to have all of the answers right now, do I?" she asked as she took his offered arm, putting a period on the earlier conversation.

He gave her a quizzical look. "You don't have to have all of the answers ever."

"Good point."

And that was that. Cowboy logic. She was definitely there for it.

Nash was still mulling over Rowan's advice when he decided to take a walk to the barn. Although he hadn't been much of a horseman, he had always been able to connect with these amazing creatures soul to soul. When he was in their presence, they had a special impact on his mind and his own spirit.

One of the horses had caught his attention, a giant mare by the name of Phoenix. She was a massive draft horse that belonged to famed trick rider Ritza Castillo. Recent Hideaway Ranch folklore told the tale of a trick-riding Ritza falling in love with Lane McBride, a New York City attorney, more proof that the ranch had some special magic to bring even unlikely people together.

"Hey there." Nash rubbed his hand down Phoenix's long, stout nose. "Aren't you a beauty?"

With his hand, he moved the mare's forelock away from her eyes. She looked at him, took him in and then began to lick his hand.

"Sweet, too." He smiled at her.

He had already decided to leave Wyoming to work for a degree in archeology. His time spent as Mercy's plus one when Doug wasn't around would run its course. But the way Rowan laid it out had made him look at himself more closely. His infatuation with Mercy had clouded his mind. Her heart was with Doug. Rowan was right. This was the time he, too, had to move on from old habits that were no longer useful.

"She's a beaut, ain't she?" Cody Ty walked into the barn with a Western saddle on his hip.

"Stunning."

Cody dropped the saddle on a nearby saddle station, where it could be wiped down with saddle soap to keep it clean and supple. The older cowboy tugged off his glove, then extended his hand. "Cody Ty."

"Sir." Nash knew full well who Cody Ty Hawkins was. Rodeo legend. "It's a pleasure."

Cody scratched the back of his neck with a small shake of his head. The years had etched some deep lines onto Cody's face, and his skin was leathery at the neck. But he had a lot of grit in his eyes and strength in his grip. "Now, *sir* just don't fit, son," the rodeo legend said. "Just Cody makes more sense."

"Okay. Cody," Nash agreed. "I know who you are, sir. I mean. Cody."

"You don't say."

"My dad is a mega fan."

Cody had taken a sponge and some soap to wipe down the saddle. "I have to tell you, I am always gratified to know I still have fans out there. Sometimes I can't get through the grocery store without signing autographs and taking shelfies."

"Selfies." Nash couldn't believe that he had the nerve to correct Cody in anything, but he couldn't have him walking around mixed up like that. It was a kindness.

Cody squinted his deep-set eyes at him. "Selfies? That just don't make a bit of sense to me. My stepson, Oakley, boy, he's dedicated to bringing me up-to-date. He's got a big job."

Nash wanted in the worst way to ask Cody to take a "shelfie" with him, but he just couldn't bring himself to do it. Then, by way of dumb luck and the rodeo legend's kindness, Cody asked him.

"Maybe your dad would like to see a picture. You and me."

"He would *love* that," Nash said. "You have no idea!"

"Well, let's get to it. Time is not on my side."

Nash stood beside Cody, holding the phone up and out. Cody held two thumbs up and stared right at the phone.

Nash checked it out, and sure enough, Cody looked like he was a hostage, but it didn't matter. When his dad saw him with Cody, he might just become the favorite son for a day or two. "I can't thank you enough."

"No trouble at all." Cody went back to his work. "So, how long are you staying for?"

"Two weeks."

"Plenty of time to clear the cobwebs."

Nash looked up from his phone after sending the picture to his dad, his brothers and then posted to all of his socials. "Yes, sir. Sorry. I mean, yes, Cody. It is."

He had always believed in the wisdom of his elders. They were long in years and deep in knowledge. He had been very close with his grandmother before she passed, and he was still very close with his grandfather, a man who was a year away from one hundred. So, hearing Cody give voice to the exact thing he was doing here at the ranch wasn't a shock. In fact, it only solidified that he had begun to walk down the right path.

It was a path that led Nash away from Mercy and into his future, where he wanted to find love, marry and have children one day. He had always known he was a family man. And knowing that was what he wanted, he had to take decisive steps to reach that destination.

As if on cue, a woman appeared, tall, slender, with dark brown hair cut blunt at her shoulders. Her face was in profile, but when she turned her head his direction, Nash stopped moving and just started looking. He was frozen. Rooted to the ground. His heart began to pump hard, and all his stunned mind could process was the question, "Who is she?"

Cody swiveled his head around, looked and then said, "That's Magdalena. She's Danny's fiancé's niece if memory serves. It doesn't always, that's just the truth of the matter."

"Magdalena," Nash whispered.

The rodeo king chuckled. "I predict you're going to end up on Danny's wall of fame. I'm up there with my fiancée, Journey. Lordy." The cowboy whistled. "I was not in the market for a wife, I can guarantee that. But then I got one good look at my palomino, and I was a goner. Sign me up for husband duty! I've been building a nice little homestead for us, and it's darn near ready. I reckon that Journey and I might be the first wedding here, but there are some that are giving us a run for our money."

Nash didn't hear most of what Cody Ty had said. He was listening to the sound of his beating heart. It was out of his character to just approach a woman and introduce himself. Perhaps he had been hiding behind Mercy for more than just time with his crush. Perhaps he had been hiding from a fear of rejection.

Nash thought about walking right up to the beauty named Magdalena. He almost talked himself into it, but then he saw her wave to Danny Brand, who had just walked out of the main house with her pig Lu-Lu beside her. They converged on Danny's Mercedes and then a few minutes later all got into the car and drove away.

"You waited too long," Nash said to himself out loud, forgetting that Cody Ty was in earshot.

"Don't worry about that for a second, son. You'll get another shot."

Embarrassed, Nash nodded. "Thank you, sir. For the picture. And the advice."

"You bet."

And with that, Nash left the barn, hoping that Cody

Ty was right. The next time he saw Magdalena, he promised himself that he wasn't going to hesitate.

Rowan was impressed. The ambience was romantic: candles on all of the tables, white tablecloths, cloth napkins, a wonderful welcoming hearth. Axel held out her chair for her, she sat down, and then he joined her on the other side of the table.

"How'd I do?" he asked her, clearly fishing.

"Blue ribbon."

He smiled at her, and she just couldn't stop looking at that handsome face of his. His tousled blond hair, those eyes. The lips, firm, and so tempting to kiss. It was petty, she knew it, but when she did a mental side-by-side comparison between Axel and Dutton, Axel won hands down. That did put a tiny amount of salve on her wounded pride.

The waitress took their order; they both were quick to make a decision, which was important. Dutton took so much time with the menu. How many times had she wanted to kick him under the table so he would stop going back and forth, back and forth? She ordered hazelnut-encrusted shrimp; Axel ordered the elk chops. They both asked for water with lemon slices.

"What kind of nightlife do you have around here?" she asked. When they finished their meal, it would still be early. Too early to go home.

"Not much. Mostly in Bozeman if you want a bar scene."

"I like the occasional bar scene, as you know."

"Our planets align." He winked at her before he took

a sip of water. "There's a dance competition there to-night, so I'm not sure that's your thing."

Rowan's ears perked up, as did her body. "Where we met?"

He nodded.

"A dance competition?"

"Yep."

"We have to go!"

"You want to compete?"

"Heck to the yeah!"

"Well, then. Your wish is my command, princess."

"Well, then," Rowan said. "I command you to dance with me in that competition."

"Consider it done."

Rowan felt like the universe had put Axel in her life to show her that there could be life and fun, post-Dutton. Really, once she had gotten what she had always dreamed of, a life with Dutton, her dreams had seemed to dry up. Yes, she wanted to be a mother, of course that was the top of the list. But she hadn't ever wanted to lose herself in motherhood. It wasn't necessary.

"But listen," she said seriously. "I need you to understand something."

He looked at her, eyebrows up, waiting.

"I am competitive." She leaned forward a bit. "Very competitive."

"Okay."

"We need to win."

He chuckled. "I'll do my best not to step on your pretty toes."

The food arrived, and it all smelled so delicious and

looked so delectable that Rowan truly regretted the fact that she was not going to clean her plate as she originally planned.

"Something wrong with the food?" he asked, concerned.

"The competition changes everything," she said. "Now that I know I'm not going to be rolling myself onto the couch after you drop me at the front door, I can't eat all of this. I don't want to let it go to waste, either. But if I don't, spinning and dipping might have to be taken off the list."

"Darn it, woman. Those are some of my best maneuvers. Back in high school, they called me the big dipper."

She pulled a disbelieving face. "No, they did not."

"Okay," he confessed. "They didn't."

She laughed. That was something she did quite a lot with him.

"But I do like to win myself," he said thoughtfully. "We can't take my best moves off the table. How about this? I have a small fridge in my truck. How about we save some of this food for later? After we *win* the competition."

He smiled at her, and that smile of his did something to her heart. It just went to racing.

"I like how you think, cowboy."

He held out his glass. "To winning."

"To winning." She touched her glass to his.

"I like a woman with a fighting spirit," he said.

"And," she said with a saucy smile, "that's exactly how I like my men."

Chapter Seven

With their leftovers safely tucked away in his refrigerator, Axel set course for Bozeman. Man, he liked spending time with Rowan. She was pretty as a picture on the outside and sweet on the inside. But there was also some salty to balance the sweet. He enjoyed bantering with her, and he just plain liked to look at her.

A yellow caution light was flashing in his brain. The more time he spent with this heartbroken cowgirl, the harder it would be to say goodbye. He'd been hurt. Badly. It had taken a really long time to open his heart again, and for some inexplicable reason, Rowan was the one who had managed, without even trying, to begin to pry the rusty locks and chains that kept his heart protected for many years.

"Someone is trying real hard to get in touch with you," Rowan said with a little uncomfortable laugh.

His phone had been vibrating for a while. She could be of the mind that he had several women off in the wings.

"My sisters," he explained quickly. "I posted our picture."

Rowan shrugged one shoulder. "You don't owe me an explanation."

"No," he agreed. "But I wanted to give you one just the same." His phone began to ring. "Do you mind if I just answer this?"

Rowan nodded.

"Hey, Joshua," he said.

"Hi, twerp," Joshua said.

"Hi, Axel," his other sister said.

"Hi, Jane," he said. "Were you together already, or was this so urgent that you had to huddle?"

"Are we on speaker?" Joshua asked. "Can she hear us?"

"You are on speaker," Axel said with an apologetic look to Rowan. "She has a name. Rowan, these are my sisters, Joshua and Jane."

"Hi, Rowan!" his sisters said loudly and in unison.

Rowan laughed and didn't seem offended. "Hi."

"Our parents were convinced that they were having a boy and picked out the name Joshua after his mom's favorite uncle. When their daughter was born, they decided to just keep the name."

"Which may make you think we're several sandwiches short of a picnic, but I promise you that we are not crazy people," Joshua said.

"And we really didn't mean to interrupt your date," Jane said with a tiny pause and then a tiny giggle when she said the word *date*.

"Didn't you, though?" he asked good-naturedly. His sisters could overstep sometimes and be too much in his business, but it was always out of love for him. "Fourteen posts, ten text messages. A phone call."

"Okay," Jane said. "It doesn't look good when you lay it all out that way."

"Actually, I just need to get this on the record," Joshua piped in. "I was cooking dinner for my family. Jane came to my house and alerted me that you were on a date."

Alerted? Rowan mouthed to him with a grin.

"I couldn't believe it! Finally! Our baby brother is on a date with a woman he was willing to post!" Joshua said with excited disbelief. "And you're so pretty with those big blue eyes and that thick red hair."

"Is that natural red?" Jane queried.

"The curtains match the carpet," Rowan said with a dead-pan expression. That response made everyone pause, but then Rowan laughed, and they all laughed, too.

"She has a sense of humor!" Joshua said.

"Well, you'd have to with our family," Jane added.

"Okay," Axel said. "I'm going to hang up now."

"No, no! Wait," Jane said.

"I'm waiting. One minute. Fifty-nine seconds. Fifty-eight."

"I just wanted to tell Rowan that we didn't mean to imply that you couldn't get a date. Of course you can."

"But his pecker has been off for a while now."

"It's not pecker, Joshua, it's picker," Jane corrected.

Rowan was laughing so hard that her head was back and her eyes were closed.

"What did I say?" Joshua asked.

"Something about his pecker," Jane whispered loudly as if they couldn't hear her through the speaker.

"I love you, guys," he said. "Hanging up now."

"Just one more thing." Joshua was back in the driver's seat. "Rowan. Our brother is such a good guy."

"I can see that," Rowan said, still smiling instead of trying to jump out of the truck.

"And he's handsome."

"Oh God," Axel muttered.

Rowan reached over and put her hands on his arm. "It's okay. I promise. This is what women do."

"He's not conceited about it. Not at all. But just look at that bone structure. He is going to make beautiful babies."

"I love you," Axel said. "I am now hanging up."

His sisters managed to yell a quick goodbye before the call ended.

His sisters desperately wanted him to get married and settle down in a house right down the street, cousins growing up like siblings. Whether that was in the cards for him or not, one thing was for certain: his sisters needed to refrain from scaring off a potential wife.

"I'm sorry," he said to Rowan, genuinely embarrassed. "Pretty sure it was the wrong thing to do, answering that call."

Rowan looked over at him with a bright, accepting smile, and it darn well calmed him right down. "I think they're great. They really love you. I'm a huge family person. I thought it was sweet in a way."

"Thank you," he said. "Just as long as they didn't run you off."

"No." There was teasing laced in her words. "Right now, these boots are meant for dancing, not for running away."

Darn it. He really liked Rowan Brand.

They arrived at the bar and went inside to see the place was already crowded. There was that energy in the room that Rowan loved. She loved to dance, and she loved to compete. And it was a huge bonus that she was on the arm of a handsome cowboy who was the exact distraction she needed to lock her constant pain over losing Dutton in the recesses of her mind.

"Competing?" asked a gentleman with an out-of-control gray-and-white beard.

"Yep."

Axel paid the fee, they got their number and managed to find a small table near the dance floor. The bodies in the bar had heated it up.

"You need to ditch that blazer and that shirt," Rowan told him.

"The shirt, too?"

"You have an undershirt on, don't you?"

"Yeah."

"Strip down," Rowan said. "Three of the four judges are women. You in a white T-shirt with those muscles on display? You could drop me on a dip, and I bet they'd give you a ten."

Axel smiled at her, and she smiled back. He stripped off his blazer and his button-down shirt, and he looked damn good. Sexy.

He caught her looking, because she didn't try to hide it.

"Do you approve?"

"I love to win." She put her hand on his chest. "You just upped our odds considerably."

Axel grabbed her hand and kissed it. "You do realize that you are objectifying me."

Rowan pinned the number twenty-six on his T-shirt. "Are you okay?"

"That didn't sound sincere." Axel crossed his arms in front of his chest, highlighting the sheer sexiness of his pec muscles.

After she pinned the matching number on her denim minidress, she asked him, "Would you rather we go back to Big Sky and talk all about your feelings? Or are you here to win?"

Axel shook his head at her, his lips quirked up on one side. "You are competitive, aren't you?"

"Always," she said, looking around at the other couples gathering near the dance floor. "There's some competition. But I think we can take 'em."

"Hey." Axel moved closer, put his arm around her shoulders, and she liked the feel of it. "First place is one thousand dollars. Daddy needs some equipment."

"And Mama needs a new pair of shoes," she said. "Boots, really."

The moderator took the stage and spoke into the microphone. "Folks, we are about to get started on our biannual Kickin' Up Your Heels contest. I will be randomly selecting dances from this fishbowl right here." The moderator patted a fishbowl on a rickety barstool that had seen better days. "And it's your job to dance your hearts out until I pick another dance. Ten in total, ten possible points per dance. Whoever gets the closest to one hundred points will win our one-thousand-dollar prize and a real nice trophy. Can I get a yeehaw for that?"

Everyone clapped and hollered loud yeehaws. After the moderator introduced the judges, he fished around in the bowl, selecting a white strip of paper.

"Are you ready?" she asked Axel, who had grabbed her hand. His palms were dry as a desert in a drought.

"Born ready."

"Me, too."

The moderator opened the strip of paper and announced, "Texas two-step!"

"Let's do this," Rowan said, walking onto the dance floor proudly on Axel's arm.

"Damn straight, cowgirl."

With Rowan in his arms, Axel felt real lucky. There were plenty of beautiful women in the bar, but in his eyes, none prettier than his partner. The Texas two-step was a breeze, so easy, he could dance it at his own funeral.

He caught the judges studying them mighty intensely, and he now believed Rowan was right about using all of their tricks, including showing off his muscles. He'd worked hard for them, in the gym when he could and on the ranch every day of his life.

Axel didn't care much about the money, that was the truth. He got by just fine. He lived a real simple life, not much overhead really. Just diesel and food. The ranches he worked provided a roof, a cot, a place to shower and a locker to stash his few personal items. But, boy, did he want to win the prize money for Rowan.

The minute they started to dance, Rowan's eyes sparkled with excitement; there was an expression of pure happiness on her face and a smile that was natural, not at all forced.

Truth was, he'd been in Rowan's boots before. He knew she was raw inside, her heart bleeding for the loss of her fiancé, and the loss of the future she believed she would have with him.

They made a pit stop after the first dance, drained several bottles of cold water, and then standing close, hands threaded together, they waited for the next dance.

"Better strap some rockets to your boots, cowboys and cowgirls. It's time for the country two-step!"

Another piece-of-cake dance for him, though it was a lot faster with spins and turns. Good thing Rowan had the foresight to save most of her dinner for later, as had he. His dance partner pulled her hair into a high ponytail, sweat making the red hair at the nape of her neck a dark auburn. He led her onto the dance floor and then they were back in the competition.

She let him lead her, adding spins and turns, showing off her mad dance skills and the sassy twirl of her denim dress. Rowan was laughing, clearly loving being in his arms, and it just made him more determined to find ways to keep this lovely cowgirl laughing.

"Wow!" Rowan took a bottle of water and pressed

it to the nape of her neck when they stopped the country two-step.

"It's hot as a jackrabbit in a wool sweater," he said, using a napkin wetted with cool water to rub the sweat off his face and neck.

"Stamina is key here." Rowan followed his action with the napkin. "That's where we have an advantage, I think."

"Could be."

The next dance was called. And the next. And the next after that. They danced the West Coast swing, the country waltz, the East Coast swing, and then moved right into the triple two-step with its shuffling style and a middle tempo song. The nightclub two-step came just at the right time, slow and steady. It gave them a chance to catch their breath. Two couples had dropped out when it heated up like a boiling pot of campfire coffee.

The tenth dance called was the polka. Darn it. The polka! That was his grandparents' speed. And he did not know it.

Rowan did her best to lead him without letting on, but he polkaed them right into another couple, right in front of the judges' table. He saw pursed lips on the judges' faces, and as the song concluded, Axel felt real bad about ending the competition with a huge mistake.

"Lousy luck getting the polka," he said by way of an apology.

Rowan put her hand on his chest and shook her head, a broad smile on her face. "It's fine. It's perfect. We did great together."

Now, Axel had to admit he hadn't anticipated this

reaction from his date. She was competitive. Seriously competitive, but what he had just learned was that Rowan loved the process of competing as much as winning.

"Yes. We did," he agreed. "Good pair."

"Maybe unbeatable," Rowan countered.

While the judges tallied their scores, he grabbed them two soft drinks. When he got back to the table, Rowan accepted the drink with a thank-you. "Oh Lord. Sugar, fizz and caffeine."

He drained his cup in seconds, then put it down on a nearby table. Rowan had her eyes trained on the judges, sipping through a straw.

"Here it comes," she said, putting her empty cup on the table next to his.

He put his arm around her, and she leaned into him just a smidge, and that made him smile just a smidge.

"I think we've got this," he told her.

She nodded.

The moderator came to the stage and tapped the mic. "Well, folks, I can tell you that this was a very close call. Let's give our judges a nice round of applause."

They did, and then the announcer opened the envelope. "In third place, number eight!"

The third runners-up went up to the stage, received their trophy and posed for the picture that would be put in the newsletter and on the wall with all of the other winners over the years. The second-place couple received two hundred and fifty bucks and a trophy. And then it was time for the first-place announcement.

"Come on. Come on." Rowan's hands were clasped, her left toe tapping. "Twenty-six. Twenty-six."

"Everyone, keep those claps going. First place goes to number twenty-six! Rowan and Axel! Come on up here and claim your prize."

"We won!" Rowan clapped her hands together, and he picked her up, swung her around, and when he put her down, she grabbed his face and kissed him on the lips.

"We sure did," he said, puffing up like a peacock to receive that kiss from Rowan, in public to boot.

Hand in hand, they went up to the stage. Rowan handed him the check while she held the trophy topped with two Western clad dancers. They posed for a picture and then left the stage while the crowd still clapped for them and whistled.

"Are you ready to go home?" He leaned down to ask.

"I am," she said. "That wore me out."

"Tuckered out and happy?"

She nodded, and when Rowan lifted her chin to look into his eyes, he could swear he saw love for him in hers. It was a flash of lightning in a gray cloud, super quick but unmistakable. And it gave him a jolt in his heart.

Could Rowan be falling for him even with her own heart so bruised? Could he be something more than a good-time cowboy to ease her pain? He didn't know, and there was a real part of him that didn't want to take the chance. Every time he thought to cool things off, take several big steps back, he was drawn back to Rowan like a gravitational pull.

Together they walked out to the parking lot. Rowan had pulled on his button-down shirt and had his blazer folded over her arm, holding the trophy. He opened the passenger door, saw her safely in, put his blazer in the back seat and then took his place behind the wheel and cranked the engine.

Rowan seemed relaxed and tired, her head leaned back, her eyes closing. She said sleepily, "Who gets to keep the trophy?"

"You," he said. "And the money."

"No way!" She lifted her head, sounding offended. "Fifty-fifty split."

"You're the boss, applesauce," he said with a wink.

"But." She closed her eyes and murmured, "I will keep the trophy." She dozed off with the trophy cradled in her arms.

It gave him a chance to look at her. She had a strong but pretty and feminine profile, straight nose, slightly jutted chin. And that lovely hair. It smelled of lavender and honey.

There was something he was feeling for Rowan. Something growing inside of him, in his heart, in his mind. But that didn't mean he could trust it. Like his sister had said, his pecker wasn't always good at picking. Only time could tell him if the risk he was taking now would be worth it.

"Only time will tell."

Rowan heard herself snore, and that woke her up. She squinted her eyes, blinking them rapidly, and then looked over at Axel, who was just pulling off the highway onto Hideaway Ranch property.

"Jeez." She pushed herself up, her mouth dry and sticky. "I fell asleep. Why didn't you wake me?"

"I like the sound of your snores. Very melodic."

"Oh!" She punched him on the arm playfully. "I don't snore. I don't know what noise you were hearing, but it wasn't a snore out of me."

He chuckled. "My mistake. I forgot that princesses don't snore. Please accept my apology."

"Thank you," she said. "I'm glad you saw the errors of your ways so quickly."

"Thank you."

After a moment of orienting herself, she said, "I'm hungry. Are you hungry?"

"Famished."

"Would you like to heat up your leftovers with my leftovers in my oven?"

"I'd like that."

"Me, too."

He parked his truck in front of her home-away-from-home, and then they both walked onto the porch, completely sober but still bumping into each other.

"Shhh!" she whispered. "Mercy turns in early for bed."

"Okay," he whispered back loudly.

"Shhh!" she repeated as she unlocked the door.

Together with their leftovers in hand, they walked very quietly past the great room toward the kitchen. Once they made it to the kitchen, Rowan reminded him, "We have to be very quiet. Mercy must be asleep."

"Actually," a female voice said from the dark, "I'm not asleep. I'm right here."

"You scared the devil out of me, Mercy!" Rowan flipped on the light to find her dear friend sitting at the kitchen table, a cup of warmed milk untouched on the table with her. Her eyes were swollen from crying.

"Axel," Rowan said, "I need to take a rain check on those leftovers."

Chapter Eight

Rowan wasn't tired anymore. The devastated look on her friend's face and the telltale puffy eyes had woken her up quickly.

"Hot chocolate." Rowan carried two heavy pottery mugs to the table. "Would you believe it? Ray even stocked us up with tiny marshmallows."

"Your triplet cousins are super cool."

Rowan sat down across the table from her dear friend and knew that there was only one reason, beside the death of a loved one, that could make Mercy cry: Douglas.

"What happened?" she asked, but when she saw the hesitation on her friend's heart-shaped face, she knew. "My breakup with Dutton."

Mercy nodded. "It's not the first time, but I've been…"

"Shielding me from it."

Mercy nodded again.

Rowan reached over, took Mercy's hand and squeezed it. "If you need to talk, don't hide it from me. We've never kept secrets from each other."

"No."

“We can’t let Dutton’s poor decision—”

“His betrayal.”

“Cause rot in our relationship.”

“You’re right.”

“So, tell me.”

Mercy held on to that mug of cocoa as if it was keeping her grounded on the Earth and without it she would float away. “Douglas knew.”

Those words twisted Rowan’s insides into a hard, painful knot. She raised her eyebrows and waited for the rest of the words to be disinfected by the light.

“He knew about all of it.”

Rowan wished those words didn’t hurt so much. She wished that she could just bat them away as if they were pesky flies to be swatted and ignored. But she couldn’t. She dropped her head into her hands and willed the tears forming to stop.

“Oh no.” Mercy stood up, came to her side and wrapped her arms around her shoulders. “I am so sorry, Rowan. Was I wrong to tell you?”

“No. I mean it.” Rowan wiped the tears away from her cheeks. “This is their burden to bear, not ours.” She urged Mercy to continue. “Did he tell you on his own?”

“No.”

Of course not.

“He gave in after I threatened to…” Mercy swallowed several times “…end our engagement.”

This was not the news Rowan had been prepared to hear. Mercy was devoted to everyone she loved, to a fault at times.

"I knew something was wrong. I did. About five or six months ago, Douglas went to Seattle with Dutton."

Rowan put her hand over her mouth. "I had forgotten about that. Did he…?"

Mercy nodded. "I am so sorry, Row. I had an inkling, but Douglas kept on saying over and over again that I was wrong and that I needed to focus on me and not on everyone else."

Rowan felt sick. Douglas hadn't just known about it. He'd met Dutton's secret girlfriend.

After an unusually long silence between them, Mercy said quietly, "He lied to me, Row. Not just once. Many times."

Rowan reached out for her friend's hand again. "I am sorry you got dragged into this mess."

Mercy was as her name described—merciful, kind, sweet, forgiving. A true believer in fighting anger with love, fighting dishonesty with honesty, fighting cruelty with kindness. But this night, there was a different sort of resolve in her expression, a steeliness in her eyes.

"I'm sorry that my fiancé lied to me. To my face. Cool as a cucumber and turned it around on me as if I was crazy."

In a quiet, pensive voice, Mercy asked the question on her own. "If he could lie to me about that, what else has he been lying about?"

"Don't be too hard on him, Mercy. Seriously," she said. "Bro code. Girl code. I wouldn't have told Dutton any secret about you, no matter how damning."

"Okay. You make a good point." Mercy took a deep breath in, gathered their empty mugs and rinsed them out in the sink. "This subject has worn me out. I think I'll try to sleep again."

It was emotionally draining. Rowan felt it, too.

"I am so sorry to derail your evening with Axel," Mercy said.

"You didn't." Rowan stood up. They were both tired. "We danced in a contest, and we won a thousand bucks and this awesome trophy."

Mercy smiled weakly. "It's a nice trophy."

"Thank you."

Together they walked out of the kitchen and parted ways at the top of the stairs.

"Cassady arrives tomorrow," Rowan reminded Mercy before she fell into bed.

"I know." Her friend sounded resigned. It had always been complicated between Mercy and Cassady.

"I love you. Good night," Rowan called over her shoulder.

"I love you, too. Good night."

Rowan shut the door behind her, leaned back against it, and the tears started to pour out of her eyes. She had been shoving them down and down, and all of that built-up sorrow came to the surface in waves. She stripped off her clothing, climbed into bed, lay on her back with the covers up to her nose and held on to her trophy as if it were an emotional-support plushy.

"Damn you, Dutton." She cursed him in the dark. "You screwed up so many lives."

The worst part was that she still loved him. But for now, at least, she kinda hated him, too.

* * *

Nash was sitting on a bench he had found tucked away in some woods just to the left of the firepit. It was private, quiet, and he could read his books without anyone expecting something else from him.

Wyoming had been, for so many years, a place where he had to do things he didn't want to do—hunting, fishing, moving cattle. None of it had ever interested him, and his disinterest had been heavily frowned upon. Now, with his sixth sense for finding bones, he could do what filled his life with meaning and joy. Bonus—his father now held him in as high esteem as he did the rest of his four boys.

After breakfast, he had taken a thermos of coffee to his favorite spot on the ranch and had planned on reading until joining Mercy and Rowan for lunch. The morning would be his. He was so focused on his book that at first, he didn't register the crunching of leaves and snapping of twigs as anything other than birds or squirrels moving in their habitat.

But then he saw, through the brush and trees, a figure walking his way. Hopefully, whoever it was would just walk on by and be on their way out of his happy place.

"Oh!" The stunning Magdalena appeared in his little clearing. "I'm sorry! I didn't realize anyone else had found this spot."

He wanted to respond. He wanted to say something pithy and incredibly charming and smart, something that would make this woman, an angel on Earth, fall madly in love with him. But the glue that had stuck his tongue to the roof of his mouth was extra strength. Nothing other than a tiny whimper escaped his lips.

She looked uncomfortable, and he felt uncomfortable, so she backed a step away as if trying not to provoke a wild animal attack. "I'll just find another spot. Have a nice day."

The woman who had captured his interest turned around and headed back into the short trail that would take her to the firepit.

"Waaaiiitt!" He managed to stretch that word out of his mouth and then this followed: "Not bothering me!"

Magdalena turned back around, head tilted to the side, walking toward him cautiously, with a small, friendly smile on her face. Oh, how lovely she was. He loved how her bangs, cut to follow the shape of her brows, drew notice to her tawny brown eyes.

He stood up even though his knees tried to buckle on him. He waited, his heart suddenly beating in the most unexpected way, for a woman other than Mercy, and he hoped he had done enough for her to turn around and come back to him.

Magdalena, with a shy smile, appeared once again in the clearing, to the secret spot he had claimed as his own. Quite a coincidence that they had both gravitated to the same out-of-the-way spot.

She waved her hand. "Hi."

"Hi. I'm Nash."

She smiled sweetly. "Nice to meet you, Nash. I'm Magdalena."

"Nice to see you." Nash stepped to the side and gestured to the bench. "Would you like to join me?"

"I wouldn't want to disturb you."

"You aren't," he said quickly. "I would enjoy the company."

Magdalena walked over to the bench and took a seat on the side he had left vacant. "We seem to have discovered the same spot," she said.

"Yes, we have." He sat down again. "I like to escape from people sometimes."

"Same."

They sat in a moment of silence, and then she asked, "What are you reading?"

"*The Fossil Record.* Published by the Paleontological Society."

"Light summer reading," she commented with a soft laugh that sent a shock wave racing up his spine.

This was something very new for him, this pull to get to know a woman other than Mercy. And, also quite surprisingly, he enjoyed it.

He laughed, putting the bookmark in to save the page and tucking it between his leg and the arm of the bench. "I plan on applying to the program at UC Berkeley."

Her face brightened, and he admired her lovely smile, full lips, and the beauty of her skin.

"I am going to UC Berkeley for archeology," she said, "It was between Yale and Berkeley, but California just felt more like me."

"Same hideaway spot, same university?" Nash said. "Life can be funny like that sometimes."

Magdalena smiled shyly, tucking her thick mane of

hair behind her ear. "So I can find the lost cities, and you find lost bones."

"We can meet for coffee," he said. And then realized he had just asked her out, maybe not for a true date, but it was the big step to stretching and eventually breaking the invisible line that tied his heart to Mercy's.

Luckily for his ego, Magdalena's smile reached her golden-brown eyes. "I'd like that."

They chatted for a while longer, and the conversation flowed without any odd silences. Magdalena was visiting her uncle before finishing off her summer in Puerto Rico to visit relatives. She would stay in a house that her parents used as a vacation home. Like him, she only had one more week in Big Sky, and then she would be off.

At last, she said, "I think I might try to grab a quick bite before Ray clears the breakfast buffet."

"I was thinking the same thing." He stood up and offered her his hand. "Shall we?"

With another sweet smile, Magdalena slipped her hand into his. He noticed how long and thin her fingers were, her nails clipped short and topped off with a clear coat. This young woman did not seem to be overly concerned with her looks, even though she certainly had a beautiful face. He liked that about her. She hadn't been on her phone during their conversation, and neither had he.

He had just never bought into life through social media. He preferred real life, real connections and real experiences that hadn't been carefully curated to convey a narrative that life was always perfect and fabulous. It wasn't.

That was a gulf that had always existed between Mercy and him.

"Thank you," Magdalena said.

"My pleasure." And it truly was.

Together, they walked along the short path to the clearing. The morning sun, warming up quickly, shone down on Magdalena's dark, pin-straight hair, and he could see natural highlights of amber and soft gold in her hair. He found her to be undeniably attractive, and he was undeniably drawn to her.

"Hold on," Nash told her. "The rain last night made it a bit muddy here."

He reached for her hand, and she took it. When they were safely on more stable ground, they continued to hold hands for a few more steps.

She looked up at him, and he saw that she liked him. It wasn't a love-at-first-sight type of look, but the fact that this gorgeous young woman enjoyed his company went a long way to build up some confidence he had never really developed. Scars of years of teasing when he was a kid were deep and still oddly impactful.

On the way to the buffet in the main cabin's walk-out basement, he saw Rowan and Mercy leaving. He couldn't help it—this habit was too ingrained to set aside overnight: his eyes sought out Mercy's face.

"Rowan! Mercy!" He beckoned them over. "Come meet Magdalena." He had already told his new acquaintance all about his friends, leaving out the sordid details of Rowan's broken engagement, of course.

"Did you leave anything for us?" Nash teased his friends.

"I tried not to." Rowan patted her belly. "But there are still some scraps. You'd better hurry. Ray was circling the food just seconds ago."

Magdalena waved to them as she headed for the buffet.

"I'll just be a minute," he told her. Then to Mercy, he asked, "Are you okay?"

Her face was pale, nearly blanched white. She looked as if she hadn't slept at all, and her eyes were puffy.

"Nash," Rowan interjected. "She's okay. Go get some breakfast."

"Yes." Mercy nodded, avoiding his eyes. "I'm fine. Don't keep a woman like that waiting."

Rowan and Mercy headed back to their cabin. After a moment of watching them, he knew something was definitely *not* okay. It felt wrong, unnatural, to turn away from Mercy and continue on to breakfast with Magdalena. Yet, he knew it had to be done. Better to make the adjustments now so it would be easier later.

"Nash! Good morning." Ray greeted him with her signature smile and enthusiasm for life in general. When she moved her head, her hair, pulled back into a high ponytail, swung from side to side.

"Good morning," he answered, setting his book on a nearby table. "Looks like I made it just in time."

"You did." Ray nodded. "Grab yourself a plate."

Nash loaded his plate with hash browns, a Western omelet, a biscuit, grits and sausage patties. The food was just too good not to eat, but he was already feeling a couple of pounds settling in around his abdomen.

"I think I need to walk off this breakfast when I'm done," he said as he sat down with Magdalena at a small table.

"Me, too!" she said with a laugh.

And there it was. Another opportunity to ask her to spend more time with him. Perhaps it would always make him feel nervous, but he forced himself past that and asked, "Would you like to join me?"

Chewing, Magdalena put her hand over her mouth and nodded. After she swallowed, she giggled and said, "Yes. I would."

Rowan read the new text on her phone. "Axel wants to know if we all want to go zip-lining this weekend."

Mercy was sitting on the couch in the great room, legs tucked up beneath her, a thick quilt over her body and sipping on a strong mug of coffee. She made a face and shook her head. "No."

"Uh, yeah," Rowan said. "You are definitely going. You need to follow your own advice to me. 'Life has to go on. Get out there and have some fun.'"

Mercy didn't respond.

"Look," Rowan continued, "I know things are rocky with you and Doug..."

"Not rocky," Mercy said in a scratchy, tired voice. "Over."

Rowan turned her attention away from her phone and on to her friend. "What?"

Mercy cleared her throat a couple of times before she said, "I am no longer engaged to Douglas."

Mercy had been with Doug for ten years. He had been her one and only boyfriend. They had started to puppy-love date in middle school, with their parents along for the ride as transportation and supervision. That had grown into a deep bond between their parents, and now they were the best of friends. Rowan just couldn't imagine Mercy without Doug.

"Not over Dutton's infidelity. Surely," Rowan said.

Mercy breathed in, then let it out slowly on a long sigh. It seemed that formulating the correct words was taking some processing time, so Rowan moved closer to Mercy on the couch. She turned her body to face her with one leg tucked beneath the other and one foot touching the floor.

Finally, Mercy said, "Photos have been uncovered."

Rowan gasped, her eyes widened in shock, and she was left speechless. Her mind was frozen as if the circuits had been completely fried.

"Well," Mercy said, "not uncovered. Sent. From one of my dear friends from my pageant days."

Rowan closed her eyes and tried to stop a tsunami of emotions, ranging from anger to sorrow to defensive to disbelieving and landing, as always, on total dedication to Mercy.

Wordlessly, Mercy handed over her phone.

Rowan began to scroll through the first images, stopping and scrutinizing them. The pictures were taken during what seemed to be a double date in a swanky restaurant: Dutton, his baby mama, Doug and a mystery woman. She stared at these four people in the photos and felt oddly numb. She didn't recognize the two men as people she had spent all of her formative years with. They felt as much like strangers as the two knockout women they were with.

"This could just be a picture of his best friend and her best friend. I know it looks bad, but it could be innocent," Rowan said, grasping at straws for her friend. "Did you ask him?"

"Keep scrolling."

That was when her stomach sank. She felt queasy as she scrolled. "Oh. No."

"Her name is Svetlana. She's Romanian."

The next images of Doug showed his dress shirt pulled out from his pants and unbuttoned entirely. He was opening a bottle of champagne in what was most certainly a hotel room.

"Why would someone, *anyone*, take pictures of him in a hotel room? What was he thinking?"

"He was thinking," Mercy said in a weak, scratchy voice. "Just not with his big head."

Rowan handed the phone back, scooted even closer and wrapped her arms around Mercy's shoulders. "I am so sorry, Mercy." She held her friend tightly. "I am so sorry. You didn't deserve that from him."

"No."

"What did he have to say for himself?"

"That he was sorry. It was nothing. Just a fling. Not like Dutton."

Those words actually broke through Rowan's numbness and stung but only briefly. "And then you ended things?"

"Yes." Mercy nodded. "I did."

They hugged each other tightly, drawing comfort from one another. It was simply unbelievable. How quickly life could change in an instant. One domino tipped over, and that started a chain reaction that knocked over everything in its path.

"I don't know what to say," Rowan told her friend.

"Nothing to say. Words can't fix this."

That was true.

"I don't want to tell Cassady and Nash," Mercy said in a stronger voice. "I don't need any lectures from Cassady, and I don't want to ruin what Nash seems to be building with Magdalena. She's very pretty. They make a handsome couple, didn't you think?"

"I think you're very pretty," Rowan said. "And we make a pretty pair."

Mercy rested her head against hers with the tiniest of laughs. "Thank you, Row. I love you."

"I love you."

Chapter Nine

Rowan had just gotten Mercy to bed with a cold compress on her eyes. The news that her relationship with Doug had ended only served to make Rowan feel uneasy about how their lives would be once they returned home. All of their lives were inextricably intertwined. Sure, she had been hiding away from social media trolls and everyone in her hometown. Her humiliation had been so complete that she needed the time to build up her armor for the heartfelt, and some not so heartfelt, platitudes and advice that were surely to come pretty much from the moment the plane's wheels touched down.

She heard a knock at the door just as she was preparing to get some fresh air to try to clear her head. She opened the door, and it was Axel standing in the doorway with a sprig of wild flowers in his hand.

"Hello." He smiled at her and turned her legs into noodles. "For you." He held out the sprig to her, and she couldn't help but smile. Whenever her world started threatening to fall off its axis, Axel appeared. She wasn't sure what all of that meant, and honestly, she wasn't all that interested in analyzing it. She was just grateful for the distraction.

She took the wild flowers with a thank-you.

"Wayne let me knock off early," Axel said. "Care to join me in a ride?"

"Yes," Rowan said quickly. "Let me put these in a bud vase, and I'll meet you in the barn."

"I'll saddle up Aquarius for you."

"Perfect."

Mercy would want her to go with Axel and put Wyoming out of her mind as best she could. That was the type of friendship they had. She changed into her riding jeans and broken-in boots, then hurried out the door and to the barn.

"You always seem to appear at just the right time," she said as she grabbed a pick to clean out the mare's hooves. Axel had already begun brushing her.

"Now, that's either divine intervention or just plain dumb luck," the cowboy said with humor in his voice.

"Either way." Rowan bent down to ask the mare for her left front hoof. The Appaloosa was a trouper and immediately lifted it for her. While she cleaned the hoof, the mare nibbled on her ear.

Rowan laughed. "Sweet girl."

She finished picking out the hooves while Axel fetched a saddle and saddle pad. They made short work of tacking up and headed out of the barn.

Axel's regular equine partner was a registered gray Appaloosa by the name of Buckshot, with dark black spots on his rump. He was standing at the hitching post, head down, one back leg bent in a relaxed pose.

Rowan checked the saddle girth, tightened it a notch and then swung into the saddle, leaving a loose rein. Aquarius was perfectly responsive to neck reining. The mare walked in a circle, a little pent-up energy that they would work off along the trail. The horse might also need a nice gallop to get the blood flowing.

Axel was in the saddle, patting Buckshot on the neck before riding up beside her. Buckshot was young, only a couple years under saddle, and he had a wild look in his eyes. He started to toss his head and prance around, but Axel, a seasoned rider, kept a strong seat in the saddle and worked with the horse in a gentle, kind-handed manner.

"He's a live wire," Rowan noted.

Axel smiled at her. "That's what I like about him. Ready to ride out?"

"Ready."

They headed on a now-familiar trail toward the pond. Rowan didn't feel like talking, and Axel was either tuned in to her need for introspection, or he was in a quiet mood himself.

The trail through the woods worked its magic. It was cool and shady, with the sun peeking through the branches and leaves. Birds and other small creatures who made their home in these woods made her smile. It was serene and what she so desperately needed.

The trail led them to a large open field, perfect for a gallop. Buckshot was dancing, snorting and throwing his head. He wanted to run.

"You up for it?" Axel asked.

"I'm already gone!" Rowan leaned forward, clucked

her tongue, and Aquarius took off. Now Aquarius was an older gal, but she still had some giddyup left in her. But no way could she hold the lead with Buckshot. The Appaloosa galloped past them, Axel riding like a pro, smiling like he was living his best life, hat in hand, whooping loudly.

His exuberance was catching. This cowboy knew how to squeeze every ounce of enjoyment out of every single moment. She had experienced that with him, from the first time they met in that honky-tonk.

She met him at the lake where they had whiled away an afternoon just a few days ago. Axel was winded, laughing and wiping the sweat from his brow while Buckshot drank at the edge of the pond.

Rowan rode Aquarius up to the edge of the pond so the mare could drink, as well.

"Damn, I love this horse," Axel told her. "I wish I could load him up in a trailer and take him with me when the time comes. Not sure when, but it always comes somewhere down the line."

"You guys make a good team. Well matched," she said. "Maybe Charlie might consider it?"

"Could be." He put his hat back on, fished around in a saddlebag, took out two bottles of water and tossed her one. "Nice catch." He smiled at her.

"Nice toss."

They finished their water, then they headed past the lake to another trail that led uphill. The path was rockier, with loose rocks and twigs that could catch the most sure-footed horse off guard. Aquarius stumbled a time or two, but they got through it together.

"This is incredible." Rowan loved the landscape of this part of Montana. "Where does it lead?"

"You'll see."

Now, that sounded like he had planned a surprise for her. Some surprises were way better than others.

Rowan followed behind Buckshot until they reached what she considered a magical place. Tucked away in the thick of the woods was a treehouse. It was masterfully built, with windows and winding stairs up to the front door. There was a balcony, a tin roof and a tire swing.

"What is this place?"

"It's actually on Legend land," Axel told her, dismounting. "Ray's fiancé built it for her."

"Should we even be here?"

Axel loosened the girth on his saddle. "Ray offered. Just tie Aquarius right here next to Buckshot."

Intrigued, she dismounted and followed suit, loosening the girth and looping the reins around a wood post. She reached the top of the winding staircase and went through the door that Axel held open for her.

"This is ridiculous," Rowan said, trying to take in all of the amazing details, craftsmanship and modern touches. "It's like an actual house."

Axel closed the door behind them. "I was blown away the first time I saw it."

"Totally!" she agreed. "I would live here. Happily."

Axel took off his hat and hung it on a rack beside the door. "Hang your hat up. Stay a while."

She laughed at him, took off her hat and handed it to him. She sank down into a plush love seat, still soaking it in. She didn't imagine that Axel had brought her here for anything other than to show her a cool place. He'd never been forward or pushy, and she had not one concern that he was deceiving her.

"Are you hungry?" Axel asked.

"I am," she said. "But it's not an emergency. I want to hang out here for a bit if that's okay."

"It's okay." Axel walked into the kitchen, took some platters out of the refrigerator and brought them to the small two-seater table.

"You are so sneaky!" she said, now clued in that he had set up a romantic picnic for them.

"I prefer ingenious," he said. "Want to come join me?"

She stood up and sat down in the chair he had pulled out for her. The one trait she truly appreciated about Axel was the fact that he had been raised to be a gentleman. A throwback from a time almost forgotten. Her father was also a gentleman, and she had always searched for the trait in Dutton but never did find it.

There were several flashing warning lights, but she had been determined to have Dutton. Mercy wasn't the only one who had dreams of perfectly parallel lives. Marriage, pregnancy, children, retirement, all of it done together. Maybe their kids would grow up and marry. All the better.

"Thank you for this," she said.

"You're most welcome."

They filled their plates with fruit and crackers and different cheeses pulled together by Ray. Rowan knew how Danny was very focused on adding to the list of lovebirds who had met at the ranch.

"Is Ray trying to throw Danny off the scent?" she asked him.

"Yep. Danny is a pit bull with a bone. Once she locks on, she will never let go."

"I can't say that I blame her." Rowan took a sip of tea sweetened with local honey. "I was always focused on building my brand. It's not easy to break through all of the noise online. It takes dedication."

"What brand is that?" he asked.

That was when it occurred to her. They didn't know much about each other. If she thought about it, he hadn't been super forthcoming, either. She knew he had two sisters in Colorado, and that was about it. And on her end, he knew she had broken off her engagement. Opening up a bit wouldn't hurt. It wouldn't change anything on her end, she didn't imagine.

"Ironically, I have, or maybe *had*, a popular YouTube channel about finding true love and designing an epic wedding, even for my followers with a tight budget."

Axel wiped his mouth off with a napkin, crumpled it and sat back. "Why not just chuck it. Start over."

She looked down, shook her head. "I guess I could." Then she shrugged her shoulders. "Let's face it. I'm a laughingstock in the wedding blog business."

He frowned at her, his piercing eyes on her face. "Well, if that's the truth, I stand by my advice. Chuck it. Start over."

"It's hard to let go of something I've worked so hard to build." Even she heard the hurt she had been stuffing down begin to creep into her voice. "Dumped in front of my entire family, his family, our friends, relatives from out of town…"

She paused, looking out the nearby window at a male house finch, with its striking red head and chest, flitting around in the branches.

Axel waited silently for her to continue.

She let out a sigh. "But I can't say you're wrong. I've been just skewered online. Followers I had with me from really early on have called me a fake and a fraud. Once I saw that tide turning, I shut it all down. When I first got here, I was posting some pics and some videos, but the hate I was getting was just too much. I scrubbed all of it from my phone for now. It's too much to handle. Just too much."

The feeling of regret rushed into her brain. Why had she just gone there with Axel?

"That's why I don't pay attention to any of that. I've got enough friends right here in the real world."

Rowan wanted to cry, but she didn't. Instead, she helped Axel pick up the dishes and the leftovers. They cleaned the plates and the table, each naturally taking one job and then another until it was finished. It felt like how they had danced, in sync without trying. And just like that, they were behaving like an old married couple that had done these chores together for decades.

"Come over here for a minute." Axel sat down on the love seat.

Rowan hesitated, looking at him and then looking at the door.

He patted the empty spot beside him. "Come on, now, little filly. I only bite if you ask me to."

That made her crack a smile. And it also made her decide in favor of the love seat over the door. She sat down beside him, and he put his arm around her and hugged her to his body. It felt good. It felt right.

"Now just rest your head on my chest. I've got a hold of you."

And he did. She closed her eyes, listened to the beat of his heart, strong and steady. He smelled good, he felt good, and so far, he was good for her. She felt herself dozing off, but she didn't fight it. Why should she? Why should she deny herself some comfort in this troubled time?

So, she closed her eyes and rested. Just as she was drifting off, she felt Axel kiss the top of her head. The last thought she remembered was thinking just how unexpectedly sweet this handsome cowboy was.

Axel was plum mad. Good and hot. The woman in his arms was as sweet as sugar and kind to boot. He liked her. He really did. It had sneaked up on him real quick, but there it was: undeniable romantic love type feelings that he had managed to avoid for a good long while.

He thought about Rowan many times a day, when he was working, when he was eating, before he went to sleep and after he awakened. He wasn't sure he liked it completely, but his thoughts went where they wanted to go, and they wanted to go to Rowan.

He had gotten the memo loud and clear that Rowan

wasn't ready for a relationship. Now, that hadn't scared him off. He didn't scare easy. Truth was, he was ready to tear it down and get on with life. Would Rowan one day be ready for love again? Sure, she would. But would it be with him? He didn't have a crystal ball. For now, he just needed to keep it light while he figured things out.

Rowan let out a loud snore, like the one she had let loose in the truck after the dance competition, and that made him chuckle.

That chuckle must have bounced her around enough that it woke her up. "What was that?" she asked, blinking her eyes as she sat upright, yawning.

"What was what?"

She studied him through sleepy eyes. "Did I snore?"

"Do you want the truth or the fairy tale?"

"The fairy tale, duh."

"Darlin', you didn't snore one little bit."

"That's what I thought." She laughed, pushing auburn tendrils that had escaped the ponytail back behind her ears.

"Time to head back, I reckon."

She nodded. "Our friend Cassady is arriving later. I want to make sure everything is ready for her."

"You've got a real nice group of friends."

"We are a dysfunctional family, but we are always there for each other."

"Real nice."

They were back in the saddle and heading back to Hideaway Ranch land. They galloped together to the edge of the lake, and it was exhilarating. Then they headed to the trail that would feed them back to the central ranch.

Along the trail, they met up with Charlie and Wayne, followed by a massive dog by the name of Bowie.

"Howdy, folks." Wayne tipped his hat.

"You do know that Danny is hot on your scent, right?"

"Yes, ma'am," Axel said. "Ray's been running interference."

"That's not gonna last." Wayne chuckled.

"Just prepare yourselves to be up on that wall," Charlie warned. "But she won't put you on the website without permission, or any of the other zillion platforms she has us on."

"She's persistent," Wayne added.

"She's my sister, I love her, but she can wear a person down."

The two couples rode off in opposite directions. Rowan was quiet. Axel had the distinct feeling that she was concerned about being seen as an official couple with him. Yes, she had forsaken social media currently, but he could see how much her channel meant to her, and she would find her way back there, at her own pace, in her own time.

"Don't worry," he told her when they walked the horses into the barn to untack them. "Danny doesn't cross lines. She is the biggest cheerleader for this ranch. She won't do anything to hurt the reputation of her family or the ranch."

Rowan seemed to relax after that. They brushed the horses off and then let them out in a nearby pasture so they could graze. Then they carried the saddles and bridles into the tack room and wiped them down with saddle soap before putting them up.

"Thank you for this," Rowan said. "Planning such a wonderful date for us. I really needed it."

Axel searched her face and her eyes, and he still found something akin to love taking root in her brilliant blue eyes. "I'm glad you came with me." He smiled at her. "I'd hate to have to eat all that food Ray made for us."

"Oh my Lord, she would have been devastated to learn we didn't enjoy it together."

Rowan looked up at him, and he looked down at her. He wanted to kiss those lovely, tempting lips. But he'd been real cautious about it. In fact, most of the kisses they had shared came from her direction, not his. The worst thing he could do was make a wrong move and that made him tread real lightly.

Their bodies seemed to be magnetized, and they were pulled toward each other. And then she was in his arms, and they were kissing. Soft, easy, but entirely sexy with a promise of more intimate days on the horizon.

He held her face in his hands, deepening the kiss, and the feel of her body, the scent of her hair, the taste of her lips sent his brain racing and his body revving up. Red lights were going off, and he had to heed them, no matter how difficult. They were in a public place and the last thing he would ever want to do was complicate Rowan's already complicated life.

Still holding her face in his hands, he looked into

her eyes and said, "I've got some real strong feelings for you, Rowan."

She didn't respond in words, but her body tensed.

"But I know you've been hurt."

She stepped back.

"So I'm not expecting anything from you. I hope you know that."

Now her arms were crossed in front of her body. Damn it! He'd managed to fumble the ball on the one-yard line.

"I know," she said. "I really like you, Axel."

Now the *just friends* speech was coming.

Rowan was just about to open her mouth when they both heard a loud car horn. Someone was laying on that horn and not giving up. They left the tack room, headed out of the barn and spotted the culprit.

A black Cadillac had parked in front of the main house and a woman stepped out of the car, tall, with a very short pixie cut bleached nearly white. The hired driver got out and headed for the trunk of the car.

"Cassady!" Rowan called out to the woman.

The woman searched for the sound of the voice, spotted Rowan and raised her hands over her head. "Row!"

While her luggage was being taken care of, Cassady came around from the other side of the Caddie, dressed in black pants that hugged her waist and long legs and then flared out into some serious bell bottoms. Her short-sleeved shirt was black; her large sunglasses were black. Her cowgirl-inspired boots were neon green.

When they reached each other, they hugged. "I'm so glad you made it."

Cassady put her sunglasses on top of her head. "Ditto."

Then Cassady looked over at him like a heat-seeking missile finding its target. She marched over to him. "Please tell me you are Axel."

He lifted his hat in greeting, put it back down and held out his hand. "I am."

Cassady took his hand, shook it while her eyes were drinking him all in, head to toe. "Thank God for hot cowboys," she said. She looked at Rowan. "You need to keep this one. Bag him, tag him."

"We aren't like that." Rowan stumbled over her words.

He had to admit that he liked Cassady right off the bat and certainly liked her support of his relationship with Rowan.

"OMG-uh!" Cassady rolled her eyes to the heavens and then put her hand on his chest. "Just ignore her. Keep doing what you're doing."

Axel smiled at Cassady and then winked at Rowan. "I'll do that. Nice to meet you."

"Very nice to meet you, Axel," Cassady said and when he walked away, he heard Cassady add, "And very nice to meet your ass! Love how you fill out those jeans, cowboy."

He smiled to himself as he headed back to the bunkhouse. He had just made a very strong ally, and he was damn happy for it.

Chapter Ten

Cassady's larger-than-life personality had sent shock waves through the small community of guests and staff. Her voice boomed, her fashion always caused a stir, and she was engaging as well as brutally honest.

"This is as expected," Cassady said as she stepped into the cabin. "Super cute. Upscale rustic vibe."

Mercy must have heard Cassady's voice—how could she not, in truth. Mercy came out of her bedroom, mussed blond hair pulled up with a clip, though much had escaped while she had been sleeping. There were a couple of what appeared to be ice cream stains on her pajamas. She walked over to the railing and looked over. "You're early."

"Of course I am!" Cassady called up to her, hands on narrow hips. "I knew that you needed me, and I jumped on an earlier flight so I could be standing right here, ready to help you through this horrible turn of events!"

Mercy's eyes widened as she looked at Rowan with accusation in her eyes.

"It wasn't me," Rowan said. "I swear."

"Oh please," Cassady said. "I didn't need anyone to tell me that numbskull one and numbskull two were up to no good. I am proud of you, Mercy. You found your backbone at the exact right time."

Cassady walked up the steps as Mercy looked trapped, clearly trying to figure out the best escape route. Cassady pulled Mercy into her arms and hugged her tightly to her breast.

"She's hugging me, Row!" Mercy's words were muffled by the tight grip Cassady had on her.

"Cassady. You know she doesn't like you to touch her."

Cassady broke her grip on Mercy. "I'm not big on touching either, but in the middle of a battle, one must make some concessions. Is this my room over here?" She pointed to a closed door.

"What are you talking about?" Mercy asked, several paces back from Cassady.

"No," Rowan said. "Down here."

"Well." Their newly arrived friend headed back downstairs. Over her shoulder she said, "I'm still proud of you, Mercy. You kicked ol' two-timing D. Dog right to the curb."

"What?" Nash had just walked in the door, and his face registered shock. "What did you say?"

Cassady walked over to Nash, the only one in the group taller than her. "Oh, it's not my story to tell. You'll have to ask Mercy why she dumped his no-good ass while I unpack my bags and get settled in."

Cassady rolled her big suitcase behind her to her room, leaving them all as stunned as if they'd been involved in a hit-and-run.

Nash was looking up at Mercy, and Mercy was decidedly avoiding his gaze. "What the heck happened?" he asked Rowan. "Why am I the last to know?"

"Because, Nash, you need to move on from me. Okay?" Mercy said, her voice wavering as if new tears were about to form. "Just go have your fun without me! I don't need you hanging around, getting in my way!"

With that outburst, Mercy spun around, headed back to her room and then slammed the door shut behind her.

"I need a drink," Rowan said, rubbing her temples.

"Yeah." Nash frowned at her.

"Don't. Don't look at me like that. Mercy didn't want you to know. And we saw you with Magdalena—I mean. She's stunning."

"She is that" he agreed. "Mercy is still my friend."

"I never said she wasn't. She wanted to keep you and Cassady in the dark."

"Well, yeah, of course Cassady. She's a Mack truck, and Mercy is the little helpless newborn baby chick in the middle of the road."

Rowan sighed and dropped her shoulders. "Why can't we just escape the drama for one day? Just one."

She headed into the kitchen, put on a pot of coffee and took out the unopened bottle of cookies and cream liqueur. Spiked coffee was a longtime, reliable friend.

Nash took a seat at the table. "What happened?"

"Think of the worst thing."

He ran his hand over the dark stubble on his face. It was funny, Rowan had seen Nash almost every single day of their lives since grade school. How come she hadn't truly registered the changes in him? He had thick black hair, a hawkish, strong nose, good chin and piercing blue-gray eyes. Her friend from fit camp, who always seemed to have baby fat right up until his early twenties, had lost some inches off the waist and gained them vertically, until he was over six feet tall. She had told him he was handsome because that was the objective proof. But now, there was something else there. Confidence. Maturity. The boy gone, replaced by a strong, capable man.

Nash threaded his fingers together, rested his chin on his hands, and then shook his head as it dawned on him what Doug had done. "Cheated."

"Hammer, meet the head of the nail." Rowan took the coffeepot off the maker to pour what was made into a mug before putting it back to fill up more. She poured some liqueur into the coffee, gave it a swish and then put it on the table in front of Nash.

"Who with?"

Rowan leaned back against the counter, waiting for more coffee to brew. "From what I gathered, it's Dutton's new girlfriend's best friend."

Nash seemed at a loss for words, and she understood it. All of the changes were happening so fast that it was impossible to process everything as it came in. It could be months before she could wrap her mind around the watershed of events that began with her engagement imploding at the rehearsal.

With her own spiked coffee in hand, she joined Nash at the table. "What a mess."

"Yeah. What a mess," he echoed. "What was happening when I came in? Was Cassady hugging Mercy?"

"It was like a hostage situation. Somehow Cassady found out about the breakup."

"How does she do it?"

"She will never tell, so we will never know."

"It's like living with James Bond."

"Truth. Anyway. Cassady found out, moved up her flight and then basically assaulted Mercy with a bear hug."

"What a mess." Nash repeated Rowan's earlier sentiment.

"Yeah. What a mess."

Later that evening, Cassady wanted all of them to attend the campfire festivities. There was singing, guitars playing, strong cowboy coffee and toasted marshmallows. All of them, including Mercy, went to the campfire after a master class dinner from Ray.

"I tell you," Cassady said, "Ray could run circles around plenty of chefs in the city. She's that good."

For the campfire, Cassady had donned bright orange overalls over a simple white tank top.

"Those are interesting," Rowan commented.

"I know, aren't they?" Cassady said with a pleased smile. "I really wanted to blend in."

Nash coughed on a sip of his coffee. "Did you say you wanted to blend in? In that?"

"That's what I said." Cassady frowned at him. "Don't Montana ranch folk wear overalls?"

"Montana shares a border with Wyoming. Do our friends and neighbors wear those regularly?" Nash asked.

Now Cassady looked upset. "Surely Big Sky is more forward thinking with all of the rich folks flocking here to ski."

"Just say yes she made an excellent choice, Nash, so we can move on." Mercy was sitting on a log next to Nash, hunched forward in an oversize black shirt.

Luckily, Wayne started to strum on his guitar, and the conversation about Cassady's overalls disappeared into the night, replaced with sing-along cowboy-style karaoke that turned out to be way more entertaining than Rowan would have guessed.

She did find herself looking around for Axel. She had sent him a text earlier, but he hadn't gotten back. And yes, she was regularly telling herself that he was her rebound, her well-deserved fling with a hot cowboy that had an expiration date of three weeks. However, she had discovered that she needed to remind herself of that at a more frequent pace. And, along the way, she began to worry about Axel's feelings. In the beginning, when she was so far deep into her own issues, it was nearly impossible to see anything from someone else's vantage. But now? Axel was a real person with real feelings for her.

And while she was pleased to be in the company of her oldest, dearest and closest friends, she realized that Axel had quickly become a friend, too. A friend, it seemed, who had failed to read her text messages. Very unlike him.

"Are you okay?" Nash asked Mercy. But before she could respond, the lovely and willowy Magdalena called out Nash's name and waved to him.

"Just go," Mercy said to Nash with an unusual bite in her tone.

"I don't have to."

"Then I'll go." Mercy stood up and walked quickly away from the fire toward their cabin.

"Just leave her be, Nash," Rowan said to him in a low voice.

Nash nodded and then stood up to greet Magdalena.

"Well, who is that?" Cassady scooted over to Rowan.

"Will wonders never cease? Do I actually hold information that you don't already know?"

Cassady laughed good-naturedly. Yes, Cassady was often a giant bull in a china shop and too blunt for most ears, but she meant well, and she loved all of them with every single fiber of her boisterous body.

"Magdalena." Rowan filled Cassady in on introductions. "Niece to Danny's fiancé."

"Spoken like a true yenta," Cassady said with pride. "You have learned well, grasshopper."

Unfortunately, this new information served to put Cassady back on the scent of Rowan's tryst with Axel. "Speaking of excellent news. Where is that Brad Pitt circa 1992 *A River Runs Through It* doppelganger?"

"That's what I thought. Way before the whole Brangelina tragedy," Rowan agreed.

"BTW. Where is Axel tonight?"

"I don't know." Rowan gave a quick shake of her head, trying to sound carefree but somehow managing to fail miserably even to her own ears.

"But you care."

Rowan stood up. "I'm tired."

"Oh! Now this is interesting. I have definitely struck a nerve. You like him a lot, don't you?"

"I love you, Cass," Rowan said. "Good night."

"I'll be in later to tuck you in."

"I'm locking my door."

Rowan bid everyone at the campfire goodnight, and as she walked away, she heard Cassady say to one of the other guests, "Nothing to worry about. I learned how to pick locks by the time I was eight. Or was I seven?"

Rowan had finally fallen asleep. Her mind had been racing, and she couldn't get it to stop no matter how many tricks she tried. She was worried and she did care, very much, for Axel. And this evening had served only to raise her awareness that, in spite of her best efforts to keep things casual, her heart had ignored the wishes of her brain. She had begun to count on his steady, consistent presence. He always returned a text from her. He always answered the phone. Her brain was acting like a Ping-Pong ball, bouncing back and forth between worry and angry wall-building. But, eventually, after an hour or two of tossing and turning, she drifted off. And then the phone rang.

She squinted at the phone, thought about hitting the red button when she didn't know the number, but for some reason, decided to answer it instead.

"Hello?"

"Rowan." It was Axel, but his voice was weak and scratchy.

She sat upright, her mind racing. "Axel. Where are you? I've been worried."

"I know," he said, then groaned. "I'm sorry."

She swung her legs off the side of the bed, turned on the light, blinking her eyes quickly as they adjusted.

"Wayne asked me to go to Butte for a swap meet. I thought about texting you, but I knew you were with your friends. I didn't want to bother you."

"Bother me?" How could he think such a thing? "Where are you? Are you hurt? You sound hurt."

"I'm in a hospital."

Her heart was already racing, then it took off like a rocket, throbbing in her temple.

Rowan stood up and began to pace. "What happened?"

"I was T-boned," Axel said. "My truck is trashed."

"Are you okay? Are you?"

"Yes. I am," he said. "I know I sound like hell, but they patched me up. Some gnarly cuts. Ribs bruised, not broken."

"Thank goodness for that," she said. "I texted you."

"That's what I was worried about," he said. "You."

Rowan stopped pacing. Tears formed in her eyes. With everything Axel had going on, his first thought was of her.

"I lost my dang phone at the swap meet," he told her. "And my brain was so rattled I couldn't remember your number."

"Of course not."

"I couldn't think of my sisters' numbers, either." Axel explained. "But I did get ahold of Hideaway answering service, and they got in touch with Charlie. She gave me your number."

Rowan sat back down, rubbing away tears from her eyes. "Thank God you're okay."

The thought of losing Axel, and the emotions that caused, had caught her totally off guard. She couldn't deny it any longer. She had developed deeper feelings for Axel than she had been willing to acknowledge.

"When will you be home?" she asked. "Should I come get you?"

"No. I'll be released tomorrow. I'll rent a car."

"Are you sure?"

"Yes," Axel said drowsily. "The pain meds are kicking in, Spitfire."

He had never called her that. It made her smile.

"I'm just glad I got ahold of you," he said.

"I'm just glad to hear your voice."

"I'll call you tomorrow. Before I head out."

"Okay."

"Good night, Rowan."

"Good night, Axel."

"I love you," the rancher said to her, right before he hung up the phone.

For many minutes, Rowan sat on the edge of the bed in some sort of shock. Axel had just declared himself to her and the myriad of emotions that had inspired were jumbled and fragmented, mixed with sheer relief that Axel was okay. They sent her mind whirling because it had just hit her smack between the eyes: this summer fling had evolved into something that she was not ready for: a real relationship. Rowan fell backward onto the bed, her legs dangling, her hands over her eyes. "Come on, Row. Seriously? Right out of the frying pan into the fire."

Rowan was waiting impatiently for Axel to arrive back at the ranch. After his call, she hadn't been able to sleep. Her mind just revisited the idea that Axel was in an accident and had made it a point to contact her. She could have lost him. A snap of the fingers.

That was the thing that wouldn't allow her to sleep. In her mind, she believed that there was a certain mourning period she would experience over the loss of Dutton. She would have a fling, give herself to another man, and that would mean there was no going back to Dutton, even if the opportunity arose. In this scenario, Axel had appeared in her life, and he was the fling. Had she thought of going to bed with Axel? Yes. She had. Had she believed that her relationship would go any further than this three-week tryst? No. Not at all.

Until he was in an accident.

That was when her true feelings, the feelings she had worked very hard to ignore, proved that they were much deeper than she had imagined. It felt as if this was the beginning of something real. Something meaningful. And while part of her wanted to put her newly discovered feelings for Axel buried at the back of her mind to be ignored, the other part, her true romantic heart, wanted to embrace this second chance at love.

And why shouldn't she take a chance with Axel? She didn't owe anyone anything. She didn't need to mourn for a set amount of time for the sake of perceived community expectations. Screw expectations! If someone didn't like it, tough. If her followers didn't like it, double tough. This was the woman who awaited Axel's return. A woman who knew that life was just too short and too unpredictable to let something as precious as love slip away from her.

Axel pulled into the main area of the ranch. Rowan had been sitting in one of the rocking chairs put on the front porch for guests to enjoy. The minute she spotted him, she got up, rushed down the steps and met him at the driver's-side door. As soon as he was out of the car, they embraced.

"I was so worried," Rowan said, releasing her grip when she saw him wince from the bruised ribs. "Are you really okay?"

Axel nodded, looking down at her as she looked up into his face. Then he kissed her. Long. Deep. Loving.

"I didn't want you to think I wasn't answering your texts. Your calls," he said, resting his forehead against hers.

"I did think that. I'm sorry I did."

"Don't. Don't apologize."

Rowan looked him over. He had bandages on his face, his hand was in a wrap, but nothing too major.

"Let's get you into bed so you can rest," Rowan said.

"I am tuckered out. I will admit to that."

They walked together arm in arm toward the bunkhouse, but Rowan had no intention of letting him out of her sight. "Let's pack up some of your necessities, and you'll stay with me."

"No." Axel stopped in his tracks. "I can't, Rowan.

I'm pushing a boundary of my employment, which plainly states no fraternizing with the guests. Danny okayed it, but moving into a guest's cabin? That dog's not gonna hunt."

"You can stay with me," she said. "I already cleared it with Danny. I told her you had a concussion."

"But I don't have a concussion," he said. "Now I'm lying to my bosses? I need this job, Rowan. I travel light, but I still need to buy a new truck. Insurance totaled my truck and they weren't generous with their dollars and cents."

"You didn't lie. I lied. And if you want me to confess, I will."

"I want you to confess."

"Okay. I will. Either way, you're staying with me. I told your sisters that I would take care of you."

"How the heck did everything go off the rails so darn quick?" he asked. "I blinked, and now you and my sisters are in cahoots?"

"Trust me, life is just like that," she said. "Besides, you're the one who gave them my number!"

"I did, didn't I?"

"Yep. You did."

Axel stopped fighting once he realized she wasn't going to give in. They picked up some of his toiletries and a change of clothes, then made their way to her cabin and up to her room. She helped him into bed, gave him some meds, kissed him lightly and then closed the door behind her so he could get some rest.

She met Mercy in the area between their rooms and

they both headed downstairs to find Cassady in the kitchen.

"Good afternoon, ladies," Cassady said, wearing an apron that read I Cook Because Hitting People Is Frowned Upon. "I brought my empanada press. Make your orders please."

"I love your empanadas," Rowan said. "Spinach, cheese, mushrooms and any other veggie you have at your disposal."

"Dos, por favor." Mercy held up two fingers.

"Done and done," Cassady said cheerfully. Yes, she could be over-the-top, sarcastic, loud and, at times, hit people. But Cassady had a tender heart. She really cared deeply for all of them even if the way she showed it was questionable.

"Thank you, Cass," Mercy said to her friend.

"For what?" Cassady asked.

"For coming. Early," Mercy said. "For me."

"Oh, that." Cassady brushed it off. "That wasn't anything."

And that was the way it was between them. Mercy and Cassady had always clashed, and Rowan supposed they always would, but that didn't make them any less family.

Nash arrived just in time for the first round of empanadas.

"Bless you, Cass." He gave her a hug.

"I already have yours ready to rock and roll."

Once everyone was served, Cassady joined them at the table.

"Here's to us." Cassady held up her coffee mug, and they all touched theirs to hers.

"To us!"

"Now," Cassady said as she turned her eye on Rowan, "let's talk about the cowboy you just sneaked into your room."

Axel woke up to the smell of something mighty good. He pushed himself upright, wincing as his muscles seized up and the bumps and bruises all ganged up on him. He rubbed his hand over his hair and yawned loudly.

He could hear voices from the kitchen. He was hungry, but he didn't want to crash the party. It already felt weird to basically be smuggled into Rowan's room. He got himself out of bed and upright, made a quick pit stop and then shuffled back to bed. He sat on the edge, contemplating his next move. He couldn't just hang out in Rowan's room. There was work to be done.

"Hey." Rowan walked into the room carrying a plate and a glass. "Room service. Are you hungry?"

"Read my mind."

She sure was a pretty sight for sore eyes. There wasn't anything about Rowan Brand that he didn't like from her face to her hair to her heart to her soul. She was the total package. How could he go about making her his forever?

"Cassady makes the best empanadas," Rowan told him. "She travels with her press."

"I really like her."

That drew a smile from Rowan. "Well, how could you not? She's team Axel all the way."

He reached over, caught her hand and pulled her in for a kiss. "How do I recruit you?"

"Keep those kisses coming." She stacked some pillows behind him so he could lean back. Then she put a tray over his legs and brought him the plate and some water.

"You're spoiling me," he said, taking a bite of the empanada.

"You deserve it."

He reached for her hand. "How do I deserve you?"

Rowan blushed and turned her head away, showing a shy part of her personality he hadn't seen before. It only endeared her to him more. "I think you deserve everything good in this life, Axel."

"Then, I must deserve you."

He was about to keep on that path, exploring the subject of "them," but her phone rang.

"It's Joshua." Rowan handed him the phone.

"Less than perfect timing," he said with a smile, taking the phone. "Hey, Joshua…Yes…As promised, she is taking excellent care of me."

Chapter Eleven

Axel awakened with Rowan in his arms a third day in a row. He loved the way her body felt next to his, curled in and so warm, her skin so soft to the touch. The smell of her hair. He hated to walk away from it. But he had to do it.

"Good morning." Rowan stirred and threaded her fingers into his.

"Good morning."

"How do you feel?"

"As good as new."

Rowan rolled onto her back. She was wearing one of his T-shirts, and he liked to see her in his clothing. For him, it meant that she felt comfortable with him. She shifted to her right side, elbow on the pillow, her hair wild and sexy. "You still look banged up."

He did have a black eye, and he'd pull the stitches out himself when the time came, but nothing worse than some days after amateur rodeoing. He'd gotten out of it because he hadn't been good enough to go pro. Bruised ribs had just been part of that deal. It was one of the reasons he had decided he was better at doing the work on a ranch. That was what he was meant to do, and now he needed to get back to it.

"You're moving back to the bunkhouse." It wasn't a question. She could clearly tell just by his demeanor.

He nodded, and she frowned.

"Come here." He opened his arms for her.

She lay down in his arms, her head on his chest, and his fingers ran through her silky hair. Getting back to work wasn't the only reason he needed to move back to the bunkhouse. He wanted to make love to Rowan in the worst way. He loved her—he knew that. And he suspected she loved him, even though she hadn't said as much. Rowan had been willing the night before, but he begged off, telling her his ribs were too banged up. But the truth? He didn't think she was ready. So he wanted to protect her, even from himself.

"How did you get this one?" Rowan was running her finger over a long scar on his forearm. She had been slowly making her way through a discussion of his multiple scars since the accident.

"I got tangled up in some barbed wire on a ranch in Arrow Rock, Missouri. I was just a cocky kid and did some really stupid things."

Bar fights, jumping off roofs into pools, dirt bike racing, four wheeling, trying to jump from one truck bed to another while the trucks were moving… Just guy stuff back when he thought he was invincible.

"Row! Axel!" Cassady called up to them. "Breakfast."

Rowan made a cute little annoyed noise in the back

of her throat before she sat up, dropped a small kiss on his lips and then got herself out of bed.

"You sure do look mighty sexy in my shirt," he said, enjoying the view of Rowan's shapely legs and other feminine assets.

"I hate to tell you this." Rowan grabbed some of her clothes. "But I'm keeping it."

His lady love left the room for the bathroom. She would return dressed while he dressed in the bedroom alone.

He dressed quickly, wincing now and again, but feeling more like himself today since the accident. His new phone arrived yesterday. Now back to the regular flow of business.

Rowan opened the door to find him tugging on his boots. "Cassady has eggs, grits and biscuits," his girl told him.

"I might grab something on the go," he told her. "Wayne's looking for me to double-check the waterers, the shelters, the gates and the fence line for the cattle arriving tomorrow."

"I cannot wait!"

Tomorrow, the fruition of a dream for Ray Brand was going to be realized: the herd of miniature cows was arriving.

"Well, it'll be a first for me, that's for darn sure," he said. "But cows are cows, even if they're miniature."

Axel did a quick tour of duty in the bathroom, packed his few items in his gym bag that Rowan had gotten for him and then met up with Rowan in the landing at the top of the stairs. He wrapped her up in his arms and kissed her. He had grown very attached to the feel of his lips on hers.

"Thank you," he told her. "You are a damn fine woman."

Rowan blushed prettily. She was tough as expected for a woman raised on a cattle ranch. But she was always kind and gentle and caring.

"Just because I'm moving out doesn't mean I'm moving on," he told her.

"I know." She nodded. "It's just…" She paused.

He sought her eyes. "I'll miss you, too. Even though we are a quick five minutes apart."

"Doesn't mean we won't miss…" she paused again before she finished "…*this*."

Together they walked down the steps. He dropped his gym bag in the foyer off to the side, and then he went into the kitchen.

Cassady's energy was both high voltage and infectious. "Find a seat, take a number," she said. "I'm taking orders for custom omelets."

"I surely do appreciate your hospitality," he said. "But I've got to be heading out."

"Well," Cassady said, "at least take some toast. White, sourdough or wheat?"

"Wheat."

"Butter?"

"Okay."

"Grape, raspberry, apricot, apple butter?"

"Let me live on the wild side. Apple butter."

He wolfed down the toast, drank it with a hot black cup of coffee and then said his see-you-laters.

"I'm glad you're feeling better," Mercy said to him.

He'd noticed a change in Mercy's behavior toward him. In the beginning, there was a good deal of frigid air blowing his way from her direction. But she seemed more accepting about him now. He didn't know why. Maybe she took a beat to warm up to new folks. Either way, whatever it was, he was just glad she had turned that corner. From past experiences, a disapproving best friend could ruin a relationship.

Rowan followed him out to the foyer. He put his hat on, grabbed his bag and then leaned down for another kiss.

"Thank you, Rowan," he said quietly. "For being there for me. For taking care of me. And for being patient with my sisters."

She laughed. "I really like them."

"Trust me. They like you more. If I don't propose marriage down the line, they will!"

"They may be onto something there," Rowan said with a smile, and it gave him a jolt to his confidence.

She didn't reject the idea out of hand, so maybe they were building something special. Maybe the foundation was solid enough to withstand the storms that would happen in life.

"Okay." She turned him around and gave him a push toward the door. "If you stay any longer, I am going to grab Cassady's handcuffs that she always keeps in her luggage and cuff you to my bed."

"Why does she have handcuffs?" he asked.

"We are on a strict don't-ask-don't-tell policy with many things in Cassady's life."

He grabbed one last kiss for the road and then headed out. He hadn't lived with a woman in a long while. He had noticed that he was kind of set in his ways from his nomadic, go-where-the-wind-blows kind of life. His feelings for Rowan, growing exponentially day by day, meant that some things in his lifestyle would have to change.

But in his gut, he knew that he felt something both special and unique for Rowan. If she became his, really and truly and forever, then he surely would make whatever changes needed to be made for the love of a woman as rare and golden hearted as Rowan.

"Okay." Cassady was sitting in an armchair in front of the couch, wearing a camouflage jumpsuit with the hem of her pants rolled up to show off her deep red cowgirl boots. As agreed upon, they had gathered in their home-away-from-home Hideaway cabin.

Rowan had noticed that Cassady did come to life when she was anywhere other than Wyoming. She was carefree and smiling! And right now, she was their vacation coordinator. She had a tablet and a stylus. "Let's get down to brass tacks, shall we?"

Rowan was sitting in between her and Mercy. Cassady always found a way to take control of the group and organize their lives. She could be a pain, but often, she took on the burden of all the planning for their trips, and it did take that pressure off them.

"We are all a yes on zip-lining tomorrow?" She looked up from her tablet. "Rowan, Nash, lovely Magdalena, Mercy, me and Axel?"

They all said yes except for Mercy. She was a hard no.

"Mercy. I love this newfound backbone you've developed since offloading that bloviating son of a gun, D. Dog, but I am putting you down as a yes. You need to do something that will get your blood pumping, release those endorphins and make you smile. Your sadness is making me sad."

"Oh," Mercy said with sarcasm dripping. "I am so sorry my heartbreak has caused you even one nanosecond of pain. I will certainly try to be less sad over my broken engagement so you can be blissfully happy."

Cassady smiled brightly. "And you're sarcastic now? Yes, Mercy! You are discovering how to use one of the best tools God ever bestowed upon us. Sar-cas-um! But you are still a hard yes for zip-lining."

It was a special, long-awaited day at Hideaway Ranch: Ray's standard mini Highland cattle were arriving. Danny had organized the event, and she had pulled out all the stops. There was a band, banners, balloons, finger food, videographers, photographers, as well as sign-up sheets for visiting with the cows once they had gotten settled in. They were small, kind and gentle, great for kids to hug and brush.

Cassady leaned over. "Danny knows how to throw down."

"Yes, she does," Rowan agreed. "Look at Ray. I swear she's just as emotional as she would be for that grandchild she's been pining for."

"I like your cousins."

"Me, too."

The air was crackling with excitement. There were the guests of the ranch, Ray, Charlie and Danny, along with Wayne, Axel, Cody Ty and many more backcountry cowboys there to lend a hand. But there were also so many people who had been drawn to the ranch just for this event.

Rowan could see that Danny was beside herself tallying up the number of people who were there just to see the miniature cows arrive. Danny walked through the crowd, greeting folks, welcoming them, but also asking them how they'd heard about the event, taking names, numbers and email addresses along the way.

Danny stopped by Rowan and her friends, made some tallies, and then winked at her. "My wide-net advertising has caught even more fish than I projected!"

Rowan had grown very fond of all the triplet Brand sisters. They were tough, strong, determined and so capable. It made her feel good to be even a long-lost part of them.

Rowan thought she was off the hook because Danny was focused on the crowd, but no such luck.

"I see that love is blooming between you and the handsome Mr. Redford," Danny said.

Why fight it? "Actually. Yes," Rowan admitted. "Taking it slow. Day by day."

"Good girl!" Danny said and then went back to working the crowd.

Charlie and Ray were standing on the front porch of the main house, their childhood home. Charlie yelled out to the crowd, "They're almost here!"

Ray, God bless her, was crying and running through

a box of tissues she had with her for just this sort of occasion. When the semi arrived, the crowd cheered, and Ray burst into another whole episode of joyful crying.

"Come on, Mama," Charlie said kindly to her sister. "Let's go see your babies."

Rowan caught sight of Axel, riding toward them in the pasture after checking the perimeter of the fencing for the new cows. Hay bales had been placed at several stations in the pasture, shelters were solid, grass was long and ready for grazing. Rowan felt a sense of pride that Axel had been a big part of the preparation for these precious lives to join the ranch.

The semitruck driver backed up to the pastures for easy transfer. When the doors were opened and the ramp was put in place, one by one, these adorable, fluffy cows cautiously walked down the ramp and into their pasture.

Ray was at the ramp, greeting each cow with love and happiness. They were red, brown, white and tan. Twenty-five miniature cows in all.

"Do you have names for all of them?" someone called out from the crowd.

"Not yet," Ray called.

"But trust me, folks," Charlie added. "They will have names by the end of day!"

"Maybe we should have a cow-naming contest." Danny snapped her fingers.

"I just want to hug them." Mercy had her hands clasped together. She had a very soft heart for animals, and she had often found solace with her pets, dogs, cats, horses and goats that she hadn't found in her own family. Mercy had been raised with very strict expectations, and Rowan had often believed that, much like Cassady, Mercy would feel safe to express who she really was at the core if she left Wyoming. Even for a short amount of time.

"Once this crowd clears, we'll be the first to meet them," Rowan promised her.

"I can't wait," Mercy said. "I just can't wait."

Nash was all mixed up on the inside. He had met and made a connection with Magdalena, a smart, beautiful, funny young woman who shared his interests for reading, quiet spaces and education. And she really seemed to like him. To have a woman that accomplished and gorgeous and incredibly sweet, and rather uncomplicated, had given him confidence he didn't even know he was capable of experiencing. He genuinely liked her. He was genuinely attracted to her. And he genuinely enjoyed their time together.

Zip-lining would be their third date, and the first date they would have with his group of friends. He'd had horrible heartburn the night before just thinking about mixing Magdalena with Cassady and Mercy. Rowan was always a good bet. She was normal. But Cassady and Mercy? Polar opposites, but live wires just the same.

While he watched the mini cows explore their new home, his phone rang. It was Magdalena.

"Hi. Are you here?"

"No," Magdalena said. "I'm at my uncle's house

babysitting Lu-Lu. Did you know that Danny and Uncle Matteo have a pig?"

"Yes. Often wears a pink tutu."

"That's the one. Danny didn't bring her to the ranch today because she gets so jealous when any other creature steals some of her attention. Hence, me babysitting."

"I understand," he said. "Are you still joining for zip-lining?"

"Yes! I have wanted to do that so badly since I've been here! I can't wait!"

"Me, too," he said. "I'll call you later."

Nash hung up the phone. He could see in his periphery that Mercy had been watching him, but she turned her head away the minute he looked over.

He just didn't know what to do about Mercy. In truth, nothing had changed between them since her breakup with Doug. He was sorry for her sadness but happy for her future without dragging that ball and chain around with her.

Over the years, he had never felt even one iota that Mercy had any feelings for him other than as a third girlfriend, next to Rowan and Cassady. So his focus had to be on Magdalena. He needed to fight every single urge he had to comfort Mercy, to give her a shoulder to cry on. She was moving on, and that was what he needed to do. That was what he *was* doing.

Over the next hour, the crowd dwindled until it was just the guests and employees left. Caterers were cleaning up the food, and guests went about their business. For Mercy, the moment long awaited was happening, and he was happy for her. And happy to be able to share it with her. They were still friends, after all.

Ray walked over to them, her eyes so puffy from crying happy tears. "Do you want to meet them?"

Mercy's eyes widened with excitement. "Yes. Thank you, Ray. You have no idea how much that would mean to me."

Ray hooked her arm with Mercy's. "Oh. I think I do. We are kindred spirits, you and me."

Nash walked along with his friends and Ray Brand over to the pasture. When they entered, they were immediately greeted by several curious mini cows. Other more adventurous or brave cows were off in the distance, exploring.

Nash watched Mercy fall in love with each and every cow she became acquainted with. He had always loved her tender heart for God's creatures. He still did love her for that. And honestly, he just still loved her.

"Oh!" Mercy sat down on the ground and hugged a loving cow with blondish hair. "I love you. I love you so much!"

Soon, more cows had joined Mercy, vying for attention, scratches and hugs.

"She has a special heart," Ray noted.

"She does." Nash had to agree.

All of them had a chance to make the acquaintance of the minis and then Ray said something.

"Would you each like to name a cow?"

Because Nash did know Mercy so well, he knew that these words had nearly blown a gasket in her brain. She was still on the ground, with a cow lying next to her, its head in her lap, while another mini was licking her tears off her face.

"Are you serious?" Mercy asked.

"Absolutely," Ray said. "Pick your cow and come up with the name."

Mercy started to cry happy tears, and Ray was right there to give her kindred spirit several tissues from her box.

After a while, Rowan, Cassady and Ray left the pasture, but Mercy didn't budge. Nash thought about leaving with the others; he hadn't been alone with Mercy since their "breakup." But he decided to stay.

"They are really something, aren't they?" he asked Mercy.

"They are precious," Mercy said.

Nash knew that raising cattle had been very difficult for her. She didn't like to accidentally step on an ant, much less see the cows she considered friends disappear out of the pastures or the calves pulled away from their loudly mooing mothers as they were loaded into a trailer. Mercy had cried millions of tears over the loss of those lives.

Maybe Cassady was right. Maybe Mercy needed to escape her life in Wyoming just the same as she did. Perhaps that was how their little foursome had formed. They were all, in their own way, outcasts. Outside of the norm, and not natural cattle ranchers.

"I didn't see Magdalena," Mercy said out of the blue, catching him off guard.

"She was babysitting Danny's pig Lu-Lu."

Mercy nodded. Then said, "She seems really nice."

"She is."

"I think the two of you make a good couple."

"Do you?"

Mercy swallowed hard several times. "Yes. I do. I really do."

"Well, thank you," he said. "It's still very early. But we do have a good time together."

"And you will be attending the same university," she added. "If you do go to California."

"Yes. That's true."

In his mind, in his heart, he also knew another true thing. He was not over his feelings for Mercy. Perhaps he never would be, and he would just have to learn to live with that missing piece of his heart that could only ever belong to Mercy.

Chapter Twelve

The next day, their group of six went to Big Sky Resort to experience their four-level zip line adventure down the mountain. Everyone was excited for the experience, but not Mercy. Mercy wasn't necessarily afraid of heights, but she was a person who generally held back from experiencing new things. It took a lot of coaxing, and sometimes Cassady just insisting, for Mercy to stick her toe in even the shallow end of life.

"You are going to love it, Mercy." Rowan put her arm around her friend's slumped shoulders.

"And if I don't?" Mercy asked.

"Then, I'll..." Rowan stopped to think about a suitable punishment for herself. "Hmm."

"Then you'll dance in at least two of my TikTok dance videos dressed as Ginger from *Gilligan's Island*."

Rowan wrinkled her nose severely. "No. Surely something else."

"Nope."

While Mercy was shy in the real world, her online persona was big and bold and fearless.

"Okay," Rowan agreed. "If you hate it."

"And I will."

"Then I'm Ginger."

Axel had been talking with Nash and Magdalena. It was really nice that those two additions fit rather seamlessly into their foursome of misfit toys.

"Hey, babe." Axel put his arm around Rowan. Their PDAs had definitely increased, and even though it still felt odd to be with a man other than Dutton, and maybe this was just rebound denial, she didn't miss Dutton anymore.

Their wedding date was quickly approaching. She believed she could let that day go by like any other, not even feeling a twinge of pain. But time would tell.

"I swear Danny would pay you just to date me if she could add us to that board of hers." Rowan smiled up at Axel. Then she lightly touched the fresh scars on his forehead and left cheek after he had taken the stitches out himself.

"Would that be so bad?" he asked, capturing her hand and kissing it.

She thought for a hot second and then spoke her truth. "Nope. It wouldn't."

They were greeted by their guides and given harnesses and helmets with other rules about shoes and weight limits and minimums. There was a short fifteen-minute walk up to the platforms. Along the way, she could see Mercy slowing her forward motion, mumbling something about being hurled down the mountain in a flimsy seat belt "cradle."

"Choosing the one with four levels might not have been the best idea," she said to Nash.

"It was the slowest."

"I get it. Hard decision."

If Mercy didn't like the ride down to the second platform, she would zip down Lone Mountain on her two legs and take an Uber back to Hideaway.

"Is that it?" Mercy asked, watching people ahead of them get attached to the zip line with a glorified hook.

"It's much stronger than it looks," Nash told her.

Magdalena added, "I'm not a huge fan of heights *at all* and zip-lining had always seemed like a horrible idea. But a couple of years back, I got up my nerve to try and it was phenomenal. So worth pushing past that fear. Not too fast, plenty to keep my eyes busy."

Mercy examined Magdalena and said, "You seem like a trustworthy, sane human."

Those words from Mercy made Magdalena smile.

"And," Mercy said, "I'm still not convinced."

Rowan noticed that Mercy was going to the back of the line every time until it was just the two of them left.

"Mercy," Rowan said. "Need I remind you? If you want to see me dressed up as Ginger from *Gilligan's Island*, the toll you have to pay for that once-in-a-lifetime opportunity is to cowgirl up and get on that zip line."

Mercy took baby steps toward the platform. "I don't like you right now."

"I know." Rowan nodded. "Just give it a chance."

They watched Nash and Magdalena go down, then Cassady and then Axel.

"See?" Rowan asked. "No one died."

Mercy stepped onto the platform and was hooked to the zip line. When the guide got the signal from the second platform, he gave her instructions. "Now, you're just going to turn around, and then when I give you the signal, you just jump off and enjoy the ride."

"Jump off?" Mercy asked. "This perfectly good platform?"

"You don't have to go if you don't want to," the young man said.

"No. She does," Rowan said and pointed to her own head. "Ginger. Let's say it together."

Mercy closed her eyes, and when she opened them, Rowan could see her resolve.

"Three, two, one!" Rowan counted and then Mercy jumped off and they screamed together, "Giiiinnnnggg-geeerrr!"

Mercy was still screaming by the time she reached the second platform. But she had actually done it. She left platform two screaming "Ginger," and then three and four, as well. By the time she reached the bottom of the mountain, Rowan could see how proud Mercy was of herself, and everyone in their group was proud of her, too. They showered her with hugs and praise, and it was just one of those days Rowan believed she would never forget.

"I want to go again," Mercy said after they removed their equipment and handed it back.

"There's plenty," Axel said.

"Faster ones? Longer ones?" Mercy had a determined gleam in her eyes. It was something different than Rowan could remember seeing. Was this Mercy breaking out of her shell now that she was no longer Doug's bride-to-be? If it was, then Rowan would be there by her side, cheering her on every step of the way.

"Much faster," Axel promised. "When are you looking at going?"

"Tomorrow."

"Well, we can get you started with the Gallatin River zip line. They've got classic or super, if you have a need for speed."

Mercy set her jaw. "I've just discovered that about myself. I do. I do have a need for speed."

"While you're down there, you might just stick around for white water rafting," Axel added.

"Cassady?" Mercy said to their unofficial vacation planner. "Go ahead and add white water rafting to our itinerary."

Cassady didn't respond in words. She walked over, pulled Mercy into her arms and hugged her tightly. As usual, Mercy's face was lost between Cassady's breasts.

"Cassady!" Rowan said. "Don't suffocate her."

"I'm just so proud," Cassady said. "It's amazing when you see your baby birds stretch out their wings and fly out of the nest."

"Cassady?" Mercy said, free from Cassady's grip.

"Yes, Mercy?"

"For once, would you just zip it?"

To Rowan, Cassady said, "I have never been prouder of any human being than I am right now."

"That's nice, Cass." Rowan held on to her friend's hands so she wouldn't try to hug Mercy again. "It's just a little bit too touchy-feely with the hands right now."

Cassady nodded, clasping her hands together while Rowan brought up the subject that would unite them as one. "Is anyone else hungry?"

* * *

After the zip line triumph and a hearty lunch, they all headed off in their own directions to recoup and regroup. At the bunkhouse, Axel kissed Rowan and whispered in her ear, "How about a midnight ride? It's a full moon."

"Count me in."

As she walked away, Axel gave her a pat on the rear. She spun around and smiled at him when he winked at her. "Naughty cowboy."

"I resemble that remark."

She still didn't really know where things were going with Axel, but for now, they sure were having a lot of fun. After a shower, she curled up in bed and fell asleep until she was rudely awakened by a ringing bell.

"Ugh!" Rowan rolled out of bed, her hair a mess because she hadn't messed with it after the shower. Always a mistake. She yanked open the door and yelled, "Cassady! Stop ringing that bell!"

"It's a musical instrument," Cassady called back. "Come on down, everyone! Cocktails await!"

Mercy opened her door, her fine blond hair sticking out from all over her head like she was touching something chock-full of static electricity.

"What is her damage?" Mercy asked, frustrated.

"She's who she is," Rowan said. "I could use a cocktail."

"Me, too," Mercy said, disappearing back into her room. She reappeared with a quilt.

At the bottom of the stairs, they were met by a frantic Nash, flushed and winded. "What's the emergency? Is anyone hurt?"

"Cocktails!" Cassady called out to him.

Nash closed his eyes, dropped his head and shook it. "Seriously, Cass? Come on."

"Oh, just get over it. Do you really want to waste one second of this place? The only way to move on is to move!"

They all shuffled into the kitchen where Cassady had whipped up her famous mango margaritas.

"Why does she make so much sense sometimes?" Mercy asked.

"I have no idea," Rowan admitted.

"After you get your cocktail," Cassady instructed, "please proceed to the great room."

They shuffled out of the kitchen, and once again, Rowan was in the middle of the couch between Nash and Mercy.

Cassady soon followed with a pitcher of mango margaritas, wearing corduroy pants, combat boots, a frilly lace top with a bolo tie and a fedora. She sat in her chair and then said, "I do have something very important to share with you."

They waited for her to continue.

"I'm not sure how you will take this. I haven't told my family yet. Let's be honest. You are my family more than my family is my family."

They all knew that.

"So, let me just say it." Cassady inhaled and then blew out a breath. "I am gender fluid."

They continued to wait and listen.

"My pronouns are they and them."

They continued to wait and listen.

"And I am pansexual."

Cassady stopped for a long pause. They stared at them while they stared back at them.

"Was that it?" Mercy asked.

"What do you mean, is that it? I am telling you that I am gender fluid, my pronouns are they/them, and I am pansexual."

"Okay." All three of them nodded.

"I kind of already knew that," Nash said.

"Yeah. Me, too," Mercy said.

Rowan lifted up three fingers. "Me three."

"We love you, Cassady. Exactly how you are, exactly who you are, is perfect for us," Nash said.

It was as rare as a full solar eclipse that Cassady displayed any emotion that even sort of resembled fragility. Sarcastic, caustic, funny, over-the-top, uber love, yes. But to show any sign of vulnerability? Rowan knew that Cas had learned the tough way as a child that they needed to build up armor that would rival medieval chain mail.

Cassady dropped their head in their hands and began to cry.

Shocked at this sudden emotional release, the three of them were by their side, holding on to them and giving them the very acceptance they always gave to them. When they had her fill of hugs and touching, Cassady raised their head and wiped the tears from their cheeks. "How did all of you know?" they asked. "Before I even really knew?"

"Cass," Rowan said, topping off everyone's glasses. "When we were in first grade, you took the suit that my brother wore to our aunt's wedding and wore it to the first day of school."

"Okay. I suppose that's one example."

"You are the queen of dual genders, a masculine, feminine hybrid. And you are fierce."

Cassady snapped three times like RuPaul. "I do work, that's a fact. And I do slay."

"You do," Rowan said.

"You are my dearest family and the first people I have told," Cassady said quietly. "This is a dress rehearsal for my bio family."

They all knew what bravery that would take on Cassady's part. Their news would not be a surprise really, but it would not be received well.

"Okay." Cassady lifted their chin and squared their shoulders. "Enough blubbering. Who here is up for some more mango-ritas?"

It was ayes all around and with that declaration of Cassady's truth, they polished off the rest of the mangoritas and then headed to the dinner spread. Ray Brand always delivered.

After dinner, Rowan met Axel in the barn. She was still tipsy and could not ride her own horse.

"No problem," Axel said with that easy way about him. "We'll take Atlas, and you can just hold on to me. How does that sound?"

"Like a little slice of heaven."

"Have I told you lately that you are beautiful, Rowan?"

"Not lately."

"Then shame on me." He leaned down to kiss her. "You are the most beautiful woman I've ever seen."

"That's a stretch."

"No, it's not," Axel said. "It's exactly how I feel."

Still basking in the flattery, Rowan cuddled with the goats she had met in goat yoga, petting them and loving on them while he tacked up the Percheron-quarter mix.

"Ray has really built a wonderful place for animals," Rowan observed.

"Her model is animal health, safety and happiness before profits," Axel agreed. "It's rare, but it's so good to see." He strapped a bareback pad to Atlas's back. The horse was big and strong with an even temperament. "Ready?"

Rowan nodded and said goodbye to the goats who loved attention. "I will return," she assured them.

Rowan put a helmet on while Axel led Atlas out to a mounting block. He mounted first and then held out his hand to help her to mount behind him.

"Hold on tight, darlin'," he said, covering her hand with his.

And she did hold on tight to him. She wrapped her arms around him, rested her head on his back and let her body settle into the rhythm of Atlas's stride.

"You're a romantic," she said, lifting her head to look at the full moon in the expansive sky.

"Every now and again."

"Every now and always," she corrected him with a laugh.

They rode in silence, a rare sign of comfort with each other, not needing to fill the space with restless chatter.

Had she ever really reached that comfort with Dutton? No. She hadn't. Looking back, she had thought that this was something they would grow into along the way after many years of marriage. It hadn't occurred to her that she would ever find that with someone she had just met nearly two weeks ago. Then again, she had never thought to meet anyone because she had planned out her life as Dutton Grange's devoted wife. The mother of his four children, two girls, two boys.

"I'm so glad that I met you, Axel," she said softly, her head resting on his broad shoulders, the smell of his skin, the feel of his lean muscular body, intoxicating.

"Lucky for me."

Axel allowed the horse to make its way through the woods to the clearing. Across a meadow, bathed in the yellow glow of the moon, he took her to a familiar place that was magical, the lake on the edge of Legend and Brand land.

Rowan swung her leg over Atlas's round rump and held on to Axel's arm as he used his impressive muscles to lower her slowly down to the ground. After she was safely on her feet, he swung off next. Atlas was ground-tie trained. He would graze, but he wouldn't run off.

Hand in hand, they walked over to the bank of the lake, finding a soft place to sit to enjoy the night. She took off her safety helmet and put it down beside her.

"This is beautiful," she said, sitting shoulder to shoulder with Axel. "Thank you for bringing me here tonight."

Axel drew her closer still and kissed her sweetly. She loved his kisses. She loved the feel of his breath on her skin, the rush of pleasure that he could elicit by the smallest of touches.

"I need to be honest with you, Rowan," her summer cowboy said.

Her gut twisted. Was this the first shoe to drop? What had he been hiding? Was there a girlfriend, a wife, a baby mama about to turn up?

"I love you."

The breath that she had been holding in was blown out. Under the strength of very potent drugs at the hospital, he had confessed as much. But she had tucked that away, never telling anyone. Not even the man who confessed. And yet, she had still managed to feel stunned by his declaration, this time totally lucid, leaving no doubt that he meant it, really and truly.

When she didn't fill in the gap, Axel continued, "Now I know it's quick. I don't want to run you off."

She turned toward him, put her hand on his arm and said, "I love you, Axel."

He met her gaze and he didn't say a word. Then he asked with a catch in his throat, "You do?"

She turned toward him, holding on to his hands. "I do. I love you, Axel."

Axel looked up at the sky. "God bless it. I'm a lucky man."

"It doesn't make sense," she said.

"No, it sure doesn't."

"I've never experienced this before," she told him. "My last relationship, I'd known him all my life."

"I like keeping things casual. And I find that a lot of women like that, too," Axel said. "But when it comes to something more, well, now, I can be real slow to warm up."

They threaded their fingers together, locked in this unexpected moment, so precious. "I don't want to get into it," Axel said. "One day down the road, maybe. But I've been hurt real bad."

"I..." She paused before continuing, "Somehow, I knew that."

"Heartbreak recognizes heartbreak."

"I don't ever want to break your heart, Axel."

"I will never break yours."

In the moonlight, with the soft sound of Atlas grazing nearby and the wind rustling the leaves on nearby trees, they embraced as lovers, for the first time, careful with each other's hearts and bodies.

This moment couldn't have been planned. It had to be felt. In Axel's arms, Rowan was taken to a place where her soul soared and her body hummed like an instrument handled by a master.

"I love you, Rowan," Axel whispered into her ear.

"And I love you, Axel." Rowan held on to him. "More than words can say."

Rowan tiptoed into the cabin, her shoes in hand, and slowly, gently, very quietly, shut the door behind her. There was a dim light in the kitchen that would help light her way up to her bedroom. She was elated, exhausted, and flying on a cloud of romance that was only felt at the very beginning of a soul-to-soul heart-meld.

Focused on the destination, Rowan didn't notice that anyone else was awake until Cassady turned on the light next to the couch and scared the living daylights out of her.

"Where have you been?" Cassady asked in their most stern, disapproving-parent voice.

Rowan jumped up into the air and immediately felt annoyed. "Why did you do that?"

"For the fun of it, I suppose."

"You can be so annoying." Rowan took a right and sat down in a chair, cross-legged, dropping her shoes on the floor next to her.

"You look mighty relaxed." Her friend eyed her suspiciously. "Did you have carnal relations with that sexy rancher?"

Rowan smiled. She just couldn't help it.

"You naughty, naughty girl."

"You're the one who told me it was okay every once in a while, to be naughty."

Cassady shook their head. "No. No. No! If you are going to quote me, then for Jiminy Cricket, get it right. I said that you should allow yourself to be naughty all the time."

"Well, I just got started," Rowan said, standing up. "And now I'm going to bed." Rowan walked over to Cassady, leaned down, gave them a hug. "I love you, Cass. Enjoy your moon kisses."

"I love you, too," Cassady replied and turned off

the light so they were back in the dark to better enjoy the moon.

As Rowan made her way up the stairs, she realized that the woman who had arrived at Hideaway Ranch, depressed, downtrodden, heartbroken, a boat without a rudder, was now a woman who felt incredibly blessed, with her friends around her, with cousins who let her extend her trip as a family member, and now with Axel. A handsome cowboy more handsome on the inside than he was on the outside.

As she drew the covers up to her chin, Rowan closed her eyes and made a wish for the strength she felt now to stay with her when she returned to her life to face the aftermath of Dutton's betrayal and her humiliation. Life was so much easier for her on Hideaway Ranch.

Maybe Nash and Cassady had the right idea. No one was forcing her to stay in Wyoming. No one at all.

Chapter Thirteen

Nash had a lot on his mind. The night before, he had said goodbye to Magdalena and they promised to keep in touch and have that coffee if he found himself in California. She was the first woman, certainly the most beautiful and intelligent woman, he had taken out on consecutive dates. Of course, he had been on dating apps. He'd carried on some long-distance, never-got-off-the-ground relationships. All had their positives and negatives, but the main negative for all of them collectively was the fact that they simply had not been Mercy.

"Hey, there." Nash had found himself walking over to the miniature cows and happened upon Mercy, who apparently had the same idea.

She looked up at him and smiled. "Aren't they amazing?"

You are amazing, he thought. "Yes. They certainly are. Mind if I keep you company?"

"No," she said. "Of course not."

"Has Ray already given them names?"

Mercy nodded. "Let me see if I can keep them all straight. Over there to the right, that's Oreo, Honey, Muffin, Sugar, Peaches, Marshmallow, Cinnamon,

Nutmeg, and Kisses. Shoot! That's as far as I can name right now."

"Ray was obviously hungry when she named her four-legged fur babies. Didn't you get to name one?" he asked.

"Yes," she said, "I'm afraid I started the whole food theme with Marshmallow here." Mercy hugged a fluffy white cow with a curious expression in her brown eyes and a pink nose.

"They are magical."

Nash leaned back against the wood fence, wondering how he had managed to let things spin so far out of control with Mercy. Yes, he needed to move on and find a woman who returned his feelings and was available to pursue a relationship. But Mercy had been his friend for years, and they had laughed so much together. They had always supported each other, and now, he felt unable to help during a time when she probably needed him the most. He was still trying to figure out the right words to open a dialogue with Mercy when she broke the awkward silence between them.

"Magdalena left yesterday?"

"She did."

"She is lovely, Nash. Truly."

"Yes, she is. All of those things."

"I don't want this to sound…" she paused "…um. Condescending or anything like that. But I'm proud of you."

"Thank you." Nash had his hands stuffed into his front pockets, fighting the urge to cross that gaping divide between them and hold her for as long as she needed.

"Will you visit her?" she asked, kissing one of the cows seeking attention from her.

"I don't know. We didn't quite get there."

After the campfire, they had taken a walk together to their off-the-beaten-path bench where they first connected. They had held hands and shared sweet kisses, and in the end, they parted ways with a promise to keep in touch. Neither of them felt rushed to put a label on their time together.

Mercy stood up, brushed the dirt off the back of her jeans and walked with him toward the gate.

"It is strange, this distance between us," she said after thanking him for holding the gate for her and letting her walk ahead.

"I was just thinking the same thing."

"We were always there for each other."

"My thoughts exactly."

"You got the raw end of that deal," she said.

"The next time I need someone to pick out outfits for my TikTok videos, I will call in some favors."

That made her laugh, and he loved the sound of it.

"How have you been, Mercy? Honestly."

They walked side by side and he adjusted his long stride to her shorter one. It came as naturally to him as breathing.

"Devastated."

"Yes. Of course."

They walked together in an uneasy silence. They had to learn how to be around each other now that the old paradigm had been shredded and discarded. Would they ever find that equilibrium, or was that a relic from their past, not meant to be revived? It hurt his heart to think so.

Mercy stopped and turned toward him. "I want to tell you that I'm sorry, Nash."

"For what?"

"I was—" She paused, then restarted. "I was self-ish. I took up your time when you should have been searching for someone who wasn't otherwise engaged."

"I have free will, Mercy."

"I know you do." She nodded. "But you had a crush on me."

More than a crush.

"And I'm afraid that I took advantage of that," she said. "And I'm sorry."

They started walking again, strolling really. Tak-ing their time, perhaps trying to find a way back to each other. Even if it was, for this moment, a goodbye of some sort.

"If it will make you feel better, I will accept your apology."

"It will."

"Then I accept," he said and then two beats later: "With this caveat."

She smiled. "Of course."

"The caveat is that I will accept this unnecessary apology if you will accept my apology for accepting your apology."

She stopped. "What?"

"Exactly."

By the time they reached the cabin, they were both laughing, and it just felt good for him to be with his dear friend again.

“Knock, knock!” Nash called out.

“In the kitchen!” Cassady called back.

He followed Mercy into the kitchen and hugged Cassady. “Where’s Rowan?”

“On the phone with her mom.”

“Oh,” Mercy said.

“Exactly,” Cassady agreed.

They all loved Mrs. Brand. She had always been the mom who volunteered for field trips, she always had room in her house for just one more kid, she remembered everyone’s birthdays, and she had dedicated her life to being a mother. That was her calling, only second to her Christian beliefs. But she had very definite ideas about how Rowan should be in the world, and wife and mother were at the top of that list.

Nash blew out his breath. “You know the wedding is tomorrow. Or was tomorrow.”

“No.” Cassady’s shoulders dropped. “That sneaked up on me.”

“Me, too,” Mercy said. “I’ve just been so caught up in my own misery.”

“Understandably,” Nash said. “I think the name of this game is distraction.”

“Zip line and white water rapids. Back-to-back and followed by something spiked.”

“Rowan loves anything with rum.”

Cassady snapped their fingers. “Bingo! Rum punch.”

They heard the door to Rowan's bedroom open, and they all stopped talking.

Rowan walked into the kitchen. The fact that they were all quiet didn't escape her notice.

"Could you please not make this weird?" Rowan slumped into a chair. "Mom has already cornered the market on that today."

"Do you want to tell us?" Mercy asked.

"Duh. Of course. I'm not going to suffer this in silence. I'm not good at that."

They all sat together at the kitchen table, and Rowan shared her conversation with her mom. "She thinks that I should find a way to reconcile."

"With Dutton?" Cassady dropped their head into their hands. "God bless that woman."

Rowan looked resigned to being misunderstood by her mom. "I can't even imagine how she thinks I'm going to, one, get Dutton to answer the phone, and two, convince him to reinstate our engagement in some sad sister-wives scenario with the mother of his child, and three, be stepmother to the child he conceived during the time he was not having sex with me in order to have his virginity reboot."

"I'm not sure he'd be all that jazzed about you having a hot rancher as a boyfriend, either," Nash said.

Nash had met Mrs. Brand during fit camp. She always gave it her best shot at being supportive, but she always failed and instead bordered on unrealistic or even rude. It didn't change the fact that he loved her. She was woefully lacking in the ability to see reality as it was.

"But even if Dutton was available and filled with remorse, would you take him back?" Nash asked. "You wouldn't, would you?"

"No," Cassady said. "She wouldn't."

Rowan fiddled with a scratch on her arm, avoiding eye contact.

"No, you would not!" Cassady stood up. "No, you would *not*!"

"Cassady," Rowan said wearily. "Don't lose your marbles. I wouldn't. But we are talking about a hypothetical scenario here, right? Would it be easier to forgive him, lick my wounds and make a plan to still get married down the road? Yeah. It would. This sucks. Okay. Big-time suckage!"

"I get it, Row," Mercy said. "Press Rewind and try to get back to normal? I'd like that. I liked my old life. I liked how settled things were. How routine."

Cassady looked up at the ceiling dramatically, raised up their arms and yelled, "God, please send a lightning bolt into my heart! If you are a just and merciful God, please put me out of my misery!"

"Cass," Nash said, "I truly love you."

"Aw. I love you, too, Nash."

"But having said that, I need to say this. You seriously need to chill the heck out!"

The day of her canceled wedding started off perfectly. The weather was on their side, no raining or heavy smoke from the summer fires that just happened in Montana. Rowan awakened with a pep in her step, determined to not let this date become a negative stain every year for the rest of her life.

No. Today was just another day, like any other day, except better because she was going to spend the day zip-lining and white water rafting with her dearest friends, and the cherry on top? Danny had given Axel the day off to spend with them.

"Sunscreen, bug spray, phone, phone charger, water, towel, wide brim hat, slides, cherry licorice, analgesics, dental floss, protein bars and last but not least a sewing kit." Cassady conducted a third inventory of their travel bag.

"I think you've got it," Mercy said, sweeping her baby-fine blond hair into a high pony.

"Just let them do their OCD routine," Rowan said. "Better now than stopping along the way."

Cassady ignored them and began to inventory their bag for the fourth and final time.

The door opened, and Nash and Axel arrived. Axel and Rowan met at the halfway point, hugged and then kissed. "I'm happy to see you," Rowan said.

"Me, too," said Axel.

"I've never seen a man get so much paid time off," Nash said. "Where can I get some of that action?"

"Start up a romance, brother." Axel put his arm casually around Rowan, holding her close. "Danny wants more love stories on her board. You aren't on staff, but who knows what kind of perks she might offer?"

Nash looked over at Cassady. "How about it, Cass? You and me for perks?"

Cassady had just finished their fourth rotation and

looked at him with a seriously scrunched face. Their nose wrinkled like there were smelling the worst smell on the entire earth and shook their head forcefully. "Hell to the no," Cassady said. "I think I got the pansexual thing wrong. I think I'm asexual. I mean, the swapping of saliva? Ick. Someone leaves their hair in any of the drains? I can't. It's not that you're ugly."

"Gee, thanks." Nash took it good-naturedly.

Having a block against anyone else's sarcasm, they bobbed their head. "You are so welcome! You actually turned out to be handsome."

"Thank you."

"Wait for it," Rowan interjected.

"I mean…" Cassady looked at the group "…none of us saw that coming, am I right?"

"Told you so," Rowan said.

"You're tall. So that's good. Nice head of hair, straight teeth. I do think you could stand to get some new clothes. Freshen up your wardrobe."

"I think, on that note, we should be off on our adventure," Nash said. "Before Cassady gets on a roll."

"I am so glad that I could help," Cassady said to Nash.

Nash grabbed the cooler from the kitchen, and then they all left the cabin and piled into Axel's newly purchased used truck that he found through a friend of Wayne's. Rowan let Nash sit up front because of his long legs, while she sat in between Cassady and Mercy. It was always best to keep some distance between them because Cass was prone to hugging Mercy and Mercy was prone to not *wanting* those hugs. They loved each other, of course, but sometimes love is best appreciated from afar.

Nash's phone rang just as they left Hideaway property.

"It's Magdalena!" Nash said, answering the video call.

"Hi, everyone!" Magdalena waved at everyone. "I miss you guys."

"We miss you!" they all responded.

"I can't believe I'm missing another zip-line ride. Next time!"

It was a quick call, and at the end, Magdalena said to Nash, "If you do come to California, promise to look me up. I am a very talented tour guide."

Nash gave a little laugh and said in a cracked voice, "You know I will."

There was a weird quiet in the truck after the call, but it was soon forgotten as they all fought over what road trip music to play. They finally agreed that each person could pick a genre in a rotation. It was a really odd journey musically, but it made sense considering their friend group now included Axel, a cowboy who listened to the exact music you would expect him to: country. Cassady went straight to Lady Gaga, while Nash had them jamming to Coldplay. Axel didn't throw them any surprises with Garth Brooks. Mercy, Fleetwood Mac.

"Okay, Row," Nash said. "Lay it on us."

"Hmm. I need to shock and awe. Shock and awe!"

"You can't. We know you too well."

"Don't listen to them, babe." Axel smiled at her in the rearview mirror. "You've got this."

"Wait for it," she told them, building up the suspense.

"Just spit it out, Row."

"Bad Bunny," she shouted. "Montana, meet Miami!"

"Reggaeton, amigos!" Nash was into it. "Good one, Row."

"Crank it all the way up, Master Nash Jam!"

And he did. By the time they had each gotten a second turn, they arrived at the zip line. All five were clamoring to get out of the truck after everyone's musical horizons had been expanded in unwanted ways. They all agreed to ride home without any music on and focused their attention on the first event: zip line!

This time, Mercy was the first in line. She put on her harness quickly, donned her helmet, and then waited impatiently for the rest of them to catch up. Rowan really felt impressed with Mercy, who had always been shy and behind the scenes and clinging to the safety of the familiar. That Mercy? She wasn't here today. This was brave, bold, grab-life-as-it-came Mercy! Could dumping Doug be the best thing that had happened to her friend?

From that vantage point, was being dumped by Dutton the best thing that had happened to Rowan? After all, she'd met Axel. She couldn't even imagine missing out on him and the way he was always finding new ways to show his love for her. Yes, their romance was just a fledgling, with no promises made about tomorrow, but she had him today. In Montana, she had learned that focusing on today, not trying to plan out every single aspect of the next sixty years of her life, was absolutely, positively okay.

Mercy was hooked onto the line. She turned to face them and then she opened her arms wide and stepped off the platform. With a huge smile on her face, she yelled at them, "Catch me if you can!"

"She's incredible," Nash said, snapping off pictures of Mercy with her arms open wide and laughing.

"Oh God, Nash," Cassady said. "Please just don't."

"Are we talking, or are we going?" Rowan asked.

"Get on it, girl," Cassady told her.

So she did. Axel gave her a quick kiss before she zipped off, whizzing down the line into tall trees and down to a platform where Mercy was waiting impatiently. Once she reached the platform, Axel came down, then Nash, and Cassady brought up the rear.

On to the next platform, and then the next until they had tackled a second zip line in Montana.

"I want to hunt down every single zip line in Montana and ride them all!" Mercy said before taking a giant bite out of a sandwich.

Rowan smiled at her dear friend. Mercy had experienced a transformation of sorts—keeping her hair, nails, makeup and clothing perfect all of the time had become, at least temporarily, not the most important thing. She was pretty sweaty, hair flying away, no makeup, and she had smudges of dirt on her face and her clothes.

Mercy finished her lunch first and then walked

around taking pictures and videos, sending them to her friends and family and posting on social media.

"Row. She's actually posting those," Nash said to her.

"I know." She nodded. "No lighting, no makeup, dirt on her face. It's weird, but I like it."

Nash nodded, and Rowan could see that the love he had always had for Mercy, while temporarily dampened by his dates with Magdalena, was still very much alive and well in his heart.

"Okay," Axel said, stretching out his arms. "Now for some real fun."

Cassady had booked a private boat for their group of five. If they were going to face dangerous white water rapids, best to only be with people likely to save one another should someone fall out of the boat.

Mercy slathered sunscreen on her face, her neck and her arms, then passed the sunscreen down to the others. Helmets and life vests on, paddles in hand, do's and don'ts explained, and then they were in the boat, ready to ride the rapids. The minute they were in the water, they were voluntarily paddling toward bodily harm armed with nothing more than a paddle and a life vest. Mercy, Cassady, Nash and Axel were happy, laughing and screaming when things got bumpy, paddling per their less-than-thorough five-minute tutorial. Rowan could not move.

"Are you okay?" Axel looked over his shoulder at her.

She shook her head. Unfortunately, paralyzing fear had reared its head at the worst possible moment.

"You've got this, babe!" Axel said. "Just start paddling forward!"

Something about his voice calmed her down long enough for her to start paddling. The paddling did help. The raft bobbed and weaved and felt flimsy compared to the rapidly rushing water and the narrow lanes that they had to navigate in between large boulders. She was soaked to the skin, water in her eyes, and she really hated it. She prayed to make it to the end of this ride and then never return. Ever.

"Stay in the boat, hold on tight, you're all doing great!" their guide called out to them. "Remember! If you fall in, feet down, float on your back."

Four of their group were screaming because they were having so much fun. Rowan was screaming because she was terrified.

"That was the most amazing thing that has happened to me in my life!" Mercy bounced up, a triumphant smile on her face, soaking wet.

"Are you okay?" Axel checked on Rowan again.

"No," she told him. "I just need to get out of this raft."

Axel held her hand with a strong grip and helped her get to dry land. Their personal items had been driven down to them, and Axel grabbed one of their towels, wrapped it around her shoulders, brought her into his embrace and rubbed his hands over her back to warm her up.

"So." He looked down at her. "No more white water rapid rides for you."

"No more."

Cassady stopped by to check on her before they went to get a towel for themself. Over Axel's shoulder, she saw Mercy, with her arms up like she'd just won a race, her eyes shining with confidence and happiness.

"Did you see me, Nash?" Mercy said, gazing up at him.

"I saw you, Mercy," he said. "You are amazing."

"You're amazing, Nash!" Mercy said.

Rowan watched as they embraced, feeling relieved that they had all made the transition from Nash being Mercy's bestie without any benefits for him to a more mature, boundaries-in-place relationship.

Then, she noticed that the embrace was becoming quite lengthy. And then, Mercy lifted up onto her tippy-toes, put her hands on Nash's face and kissed him. Right there in public, in front of God and everybody. She planted a big ol' kiss on Nash, not a peck.

"Did I just see Mercy Adams kiss Nash Landry?" Cassady asked, stunned.

Rowan's response was a sigh.

"What's the problem?" Axel asked. "They're both single."

"This is why I am permanently single, by choice," Cassady said. "You all are just messy."

Chapter Fourteen

The ride home from the white water rafting was quiet; even Cassady didn't speak. Yes, everyone was tired, but Mercy knew that the kiss she had given Nash had shocked everyone, and she had to include herself in that category, as well. In the silence, she had time to really think about her spontaneous romantic embrace with a young man who had been her confidant, best friend and shoulder to cry on for nearly two decades.

Not even once in their relationship had she considered Nash any more than just a friend. Of course it had been flattering to know someone in the world idolized her, just as she knew that Rowan was correct—with her impending wedding the following year, Mercy had to let Nash go.

It had been difficult. She missed him. And if she were perfectly honest with herself and no one else, she had felt jealous when she saw Nash with Magdalena. She forced herself to keep that under wraps, never letting on to anyone in the friend group, because, she had to face it, she didn't have one leg to stand on in that arena.

And then today, she had just felt so free, so powerful, so energized by her newfound bravery and embrace of life and taking a walk on the wild side, that in a moment of exuberance, she planted a big ol' wet one on Nash.

That was a head-scratcher for sure.

"Back to paradise." Axel pulled onto Hideaway Ranch Way, newly christened by the triplets.

When he pulled into a parking spot and shut off the engine, he looked around at the four of them. "Now, you guys are usually talking a mile a minute, talking over each other and loud. Lord Jesus, so loud! But what y'all are doin' right here? That's creeping me out. For cryin' out loud, just fix it. Be normal."

"Your hot cowboy isn't wrong," Cassady conceded. "Mercy shoving her tongue down Nash's throat screwed up our mojo."

"It wasn't a French kiss," Nash said, turning his body toward the back seat.

"Does that really matter?" Rowan asked.

"Well, yes," he said. "It's a misrepresentation of the event that transpired."

"Nash," Cassady said, "if you don't stop playing knight in shining armor to Mercy's damsel in distress, I am going to take off my brand-new pair of Stevie High Beep wedges and hit you with them."

Axel had walked around to the passenger side of his truck to get Rowan. When he opened the door, Mercy, Cassady and Nash were in a heated discussion about assault by shoe. "Scratch everything I just said," Axel amended. "Quiet is way better."

Rowan was staring straight ahead, tuning out everyone. Looking at something. Or someone. Her stomach felt queasy, and a migraine appeared out of nowhere. For a second that seemed way longer, she felt dizzy. Woozy. Parched.

"Dutton." She tried to speak loud enough to break through the noise, but her voice was scratchy and weak.

"What'd you say? Dutton?" Axel asked loud and clear, following her gaze to the front porch.

"Dutton?" Cassady, Mercy and Nash all asked in stereo, looking around.

"Dutton," Rowan repeated with a nod to the porch.

"And Douglas," Mercy added in a near whisper. "And Douglas."

"But of course," Nash said. "Where there's one, there's two."

Dutton looked handsome. Dressed to impress with dark wash jeans, a new Stetson, an aqua blue shirt—her favorite color—blazer and dress boots shined to a high polish. He didn't have Axel's rugged looks, but he turned heads.

Now, the sight of him made Rowan feel nauseated. She had systematically scrubbed Dutton from her life. On nights when she couldn't sleep trying to make sense of things, she deleted pictures of him. She blocked him and Douglas from her socials, and she hadn't even sneaked a peek at her online life because Dutton and she had too many mutual friends and relatives to ever be out of each other's lives for good. But for now, not seeing his stupid, lying, cheating face made life easier.

The four of them got out of Axel's truck, and Douglas looked at Mercy with a sheepish expression as he tipped his hat to her. That boy was rich in charm if poor in substance.

Thick as thieves, Douglas and Dutton each picked up over-the-top bouquets of flowers and walked down the porch steps together. Cocky. They were used to smoothing things over with some flowers and a fancy meal. But that wasn't going to work this time. Not this time.

"You've got some giant round ones, Dutton, I will grant you that," Cassady said. "Showing up *today* of all days."

Dutton ignored everyone and trained his entire being on Rowan. She could feel Axel beside her, the energy off his body ramping up. He was a natural protector, but he was also confident, calculating. He wasn't a live wire like Dutton. Underneath all of that calm exterior, Dutton had a quick temper.

"I know you aren't happy to see me, Rowan," Dutton said. "But I'm happy to see you."

She was speechless. Not one word to say entered her mind. Shock was all she could figure. She was in total shock.

Dutton took another cautious step toward her. "Is there someplace we can have a private talk?"

Rowan nodded. "Our cabin."

Rowan was aware that Douglas had approached Mercy and offered her the flowers, which she did not accept. Cassady came with them, while Nash stayed behind, hands in his pockets and a concerned expression on his face.

"Are you okay?" Axel had stayed with Rowan.

She nodded. "I'll fill you in later."

"I'm close by if you need me."

She gave him another nod. In that moment, the stark contrast between Dutton and Axel was so easy to see. Axel hadn't hung all over her or made a PDA, stepping up to stake his claim. No. He was a confident, self-assured man who loved her enough and respected her enough to let her handle her business. Unlike Dutton, whose neck was starting to turn red, a sure sign he was getting steamed.

"I'll get these in water," Cassady said, taking the bouquets of flowers. "It's not their fault you two are twits."

Dutton took off his hat and hung it on the rack in the foyer, as did Douglas.

"It's mighty fine." Her ex-fiancé looked around.

"It is." Rowan nodded with a sense of dysphoria. Dutton was here. Douglas was here. Uninvited. Their presence unwelcome.

"Second that," Douglas said, rocking back and forth on his heels. "Real fine."

Rowan exchanged a look with Mercy, and there was a steeliness in her gaze that Rowan had never seen. Mercy had been raised to be a supportive and excellent wife and devoted mother. Some might think it was old-fashioned or backward. That wasn't to say that Mercy didn't have free will; she did. She never chose to use it.

There was a smile inside of Rowan's mind that didn't

make it to her expression. Something was telling her that Douglas was about to meet a zip-lining, white water rafting, having the occasional spiked beverage in the afternoon, daredevil Mercy. He was in for a surprise.

"Let's head upstairs," Rowan said.

At the second-floor landing, Dutton followed her into her room and Douglas followed Mercy into hers. Once inside, Rowan shut the door and stayed facing it for a second or two, still trying to get a grip on the whole moment she found herself in. This was to be her wedding day. This was to be the day that she was to become Dutton Grange's wife.

She turned around, leaned back against the door and stared at him, but right through him.

"Montana agrees with you, Row." Dutton took off his blazer, hung it up on one of the hangers in the closet, unbuttoned his cuffs and rolled up the sleeves. "Do you mind?" He gestured to the bed.

"Not at all."

In pure Dutton fashion, he jumped and landed on the bed, leaning back against the pillows, his ankles crossed casually.

"Nice mattress." He bounced a little with a smile and a wink. "Firm."

She stared at him, and when she didn't return his smile or volley back his attempt at humor, he got up and sat down properly on the edge of the bed.

She had taken a seat at the small café table in a nook meant for reading or writing or enjoying the glorious views.

"Do you hate me?" He jumped right into it. That was his style. She still admired him for that.

"I did." She folded her hands, one on top of the other, and then rested them on her knees.

"You're the forgiving type," Dutton said and added sincerely, "The sign of a good woman. A great woman."

How had she, in such a short time, become impervious to Dutton's charm? She hadn't known that about herself until just this minute. She cleared her throat and asked, "Why are you here?"

He looked at her, trying to gauge her. "Damn it, Row. I just screwed up. I mean, I screwed up big time."

She let him keep talking.

He ran his hand over his recently trimmed dark hair several times. It was a stall tactic she had seen him use for years. Perhaps this wasn't going exactly as he had believed it would. Dutton stood up, shoved his hands into his pockets and looked at her square. "I want you back, honey. I don't deserve you. I know that. But I truly love you. I do."

Nothing came to mind to say, so she remained quiet.

"This is our wedding day, sweetheart."

"Was." That felt like a knife in the gut.

He looked down, shook his head and said, "I know. I know. I was an idiot. I still am, truth be told. I'm a bona fide idiot, I'm sure you would agree with that. Hell! Cassady and I can finally agree on something."

Dutton was trying to build a bond with her by calling himself all of the names he assumed she had called him. A sign that he was feeling insecure about his strategy.

"Now, sweetheart, don't get mad. But I did talk to your mama, and she suggested that—"

One little spark and the entire powder keg went boom.

Rowan jumped up, marched over to him and poked him in the chest with her finger to emphasize every single word. "How dare you talk to my mom about me! You do not have that right! You. Do. Not. Have. That. Right!"

She strode back to the café table, but was too angry to sit down. "How dare you, Dutton! How dare you! The last time I checked, you broke off our engagement *at our rehearsal* because you got a woman in Seattle pregnant! Immaculate conception, was it? You being a born-again virgin and all."

Dutton rubbed the back of his neck and said in an aw-shucks voice, "No. No. But I don't really know that it's mine. Turns out, there might just be another fish on that hook. The minute the doctor slaps that baby on the behind, paternity test. And honestly, Row, she isn't you. She's high-strung. Needy. Not like you. You're just so nurturing."

Rowan stood with her feet planted apart, her hands at her waist, looking at Dutton with narrowed eyes. She had wanted to keep the tears at bay, not giving him the satisfaction to see her cry. But the tears started to stream out of her eyes. She wasn't sobbing or blubbering… The tears were just the manifestation of all of the pain and anguish she had stuffed down to the very bottom of her soul.

"You humiliated me. You lied to me. You cheated on me. You betrayed me. You broke my heart."

"I know, Row. I'm sorry."

"You don't get to say you're sorry to me," she said in a seething voice, tears still falling onto her cheeks, her chin, down her neck, onto her shirt. She didn't wipe them away. "I loved you, Dutton."

"I know. And I didn't deserve you. But I want to try to deserve you, honey. Let me try. Please let me try."

Her voice went cold. "There is a part of me that will always love you."

Dutton thought he saw an opening. He took a step toward her, shoulders rolled forward a bit, hands clasped in a prayer pose. "I will always love you, Row. Just please give me one more chance. Just one, and I promise you, I will be the man you deserve."

Rowan wiped the tears off her face with the back of her forearm as she sat down. "Why, Dutton? For what purpose? I'm nothing to you."

"God blast it. I'm trying here. Why can't you meet me halfway?" Dutton sat down heavily on the bed and put his head in his hands.

In that moment, she was able to read her ex-fiancé more clearly than she ever had before. When it came to his parents, he was weak. They wanted him to marry her, so he was here. Trying to get her back.

"You know what?" she said in a removed voice, her eyes looking down at the wood floor. "I saw pictures of that woman in Seattle. She is beautiful."

Dutton lifted up his eyes, and so did she. Their eyes locked.

"If that baby is yours, Dutton, do the right thing by them. The mother and the child," she said. "I don't believe for one second that there's a long list of sperm donors. That's just you trying to shift blame for your own actions."

Dutton's face fell. He suddenly looked tired. Deflated.

"This is done," she said. "This is finished."

Dutton stood up, walked over to her, pulled something out of his pocket and offered it to her. "Please, Row. Just think about it. Don't make a decision right now."

"Time won't change my mind," she said, feeling a deep sense of sadness and loss. "That's your grandmother's ring. I can't accept that. I loved your nana."

Dutton held the ring in his fingers, head bowed, emotion in his voice. "She loved you. She truly did."

She stood up, walked over to him, and she hugged him. He wrapped his arms around her and hung on tightly.

"Is this about that cowboy?" he asked, still holding on to her.

Same ol' Dutton.

Rowan pushed away. "This is about me. Not anyone else. I discovered how to love myself, Dutton. I figured out that I don't need to be anyone's wife to feel like I matter. So, no. This isn't about another man. This is about me, loving myself, seeing the value I have without anyone beside me. I don't have to be anyone's wife to feel whole."

And with that, Dutton rolled down his sleeves, re-buttoned the cuffs, took his blazer off the hanger and slipped it on slowly.

He looked at her. "I do wish you the best, Row. I really do."

"I wish you the best, too," she said. "Let's face it, we are going to see a lot of each other. May as well decide to be cordial now."

He nodded wordlessly as he opened the door.

As they both stepped out of her room, Mercy's door swung open and banged against the doorjamb.

"No. No. No. No. No. No. NO!" Mercy said. "I am not going to marry you, Douglas, not now, not ever! You wanted to get caught! You wanted out, and you didn't have the guts to say it to my face or say it to your parents!"

"Come on," Douglas said. "Why would I go and do something stupid like that? That doesn't even make good sense."

"If you didn't want to get caught, perhaps not taking a selfie with a woman in a hotel room would have been a good place to start," Mercy said, hands on her hips, her eyes flashing. "You did me a favor, Douglas. You did."

"Aw, damn it, Mercy. What do I have to do to get us back on track? What present do you need? A black Visa card? A new car? Trips abroad? What? Whatever it is, just tell me, and it will be yours."

Mercy didn't say a word for enough time that it started to feel as if someone should fill the space with something.

"Listen to me very closely, Douglas," she said at last.

Her voice was very low, so controlled that Rowan had to actively listen to hear her. “I don’t want anything from you other than to leave me alone. Don’t call me. Don’t text me. Don’t send an email. Don’t stalk me on social media. Don’t send a carrier pigeon. And for the love of peanuts, don’t send me flowers. Or candy. Or jewelry.”

“So what are you saying?” Douglas smirked and looked over at Dutton for some bro support. “That we’re done-zo?”

“Yes,” Mercy said. “We are most definitely done-zo.”

There was another odd silence where it seemed that the four of them weren’t exactly sure where to put the period on this encounter. Coming up from the bottom floor, they heard a noise that sounded like someone trying very hard to hold in their emotions.

Cassady appeared at the bottom of the stairwell, their eyes teary, their hands together, resting on their chin. “I am not sorry to interrupt. I never am.” They beamed at Mercy. “I just can’t hold this in for another second of my life. Mercy? I am so proud of you.”

“Thank you,” Mercy said.

“You are my precious, delicate baby bird who grew into a pterodactyl.” Cassady pulled tissues out of their bra and dabbed at their eyes.

“I’m out of here,” Douglas snapped and then pointed at Mercy. “You’ll regret this.”

Dutton followed Douglas, and Cassady met them at the door, handing each hat to its owner in their most polite, deferential, host-with-the-most persona.

Dutton put his hat on and said to Cassady, "I never did like you."

"Likewise, I'm sure."

Dutton turned toward Rowan. "Goodbye, Row."

"Goodbye, Dutton," she said and then added, "I forgive you."

Her first love let that sink in and then said sincerely, "Thank you for that, I guess."

"Okay, let's wrap this up now." Cassady opened the door, waving them along with their hand. "Don't let the door hit ya where the good Lord split ya." They shut the door, did a pirouette, bowed and said, "We deserve an adult beverage."

Rowan hugged Mercy tightly, and then they headed to the kitchen for that promised adult beverage in celebration of the end of her relationship with Dutton on a day that would have been her wedding day. As a bonus, Mercy got the chance to send Douglas packing, too.

Some days were just better than others.

Rowan walked onto the front porch of their cabin. She felt at peace. There was a cool breeze and a crispness in the Montana air that suited her. Perhaps this final goodbye with Dutton was the thing she needed to move on. There had been so many emotions, all over the map and in opposition to each other, with everything jumbled up and sloshed together, that she had refused to feel.

She got the opportunity to give voice to those emotions and let them dissolve into the ether, like the sun burning off the fog. Dutton hadn't intended to give her this gift, but he had.

"I'm sorry I couldn't get here sooner. One of the seasonal cowpokes got one of our tractors stuck but good, right next to steep embankment of all the rotten luck. Damn near lost the machine," Axel explained when he reached her and wrapped her in his arms. "I promised to be close by and then I got an SOS. I had to answer that call."

"Of course you did."

"Are you okay?" He leaned back so he could look into her eyes.

She had texted him that Dutton was gone and nodded, burying her head in his chest, breathing him in.

Together, they sat close on the porch swing, his arm around her.

"Thank you," she said at last.

"What for?"

She looked up at his face. "For trusting me. For believing in me."

"That's a given."

"Not always."

"Do you want to tell me about it?"

"I do," she said softly. "We said goodbye."

"He didn't look like he was looking for goodbye with that flower shop he brought with him." Axel was joking, but she could hear just a sliver of doubt in his voice. Of course, he would feel off-kilter. What they had was brand-new. But for her, it was more real than anything she had ever felt before.

"This was going to be our wedding day."

She felt Axel's body tense next to her. "So that's why he showed up. Hat in hand. Babe, that's awful."

She nodded. She reached over, took his free hand in hers and said, "I need to tell you something. Everything happened so fast. One day I woke up, and my whole entire life, the one I had so faithfully built, was gone. Because I built my foundation on shifting sand." She stopped, cleared her throat and continued, "In my community, I was known as Dutton's girlfriend. Then, Dutton's fiancée. And today, I was going to be Dutton's wife." She breathed in and let it out slowly. "And then I come here and meet you."

He pulled her close and kissed the top of her head.

"But I can't keep this from you, Axel. It wouldn't be fair. Even though we haven't made any promises, we are just beginning, really."

"Tell me," he said. "It's okay."

She looked at him. "I had thought about going back to Dutton. Forgive him and go back. I knew before he showed up here that he would take me back. But I just couldn't. I couldn't. I am sorry if you think I misled you."

"Hey," Axel said. "You don't have to apologize to me, Rowan. I love you. That's the truth of the matter."

"I don't have anything figured out about next week or next month or next year." She caught his gaze and held it. "But I do know that I love you, too. And that's just the truth of the matter."

Chapter Fifteen

The day after Dutton and Douglas had been given their marching orders, Rowan and Mercy took a much-needed goat yoga class. Together with nearly twenty other attendees, they attempted to follow Ray's instructions to twist and contort into shapes and poses that seemed entirely unfair to their bodies. Downward Facing Dog became Downward Facing Don't.

Rowan was flat on the mat enjoying lying-on-my-back pose, when a tiny baby goat by the name of Petunia sat down on her stomach. The tan-and-white fluffball looked down at her with the most beautiful blue eyes.

"You get it, Petunia, don't you?" Rowan asked. She glanced over at Mercy, who was executing the lying-on-my-stomach pose. An all-black goat with a dot of white between its eyes had taken up residence on her back.

"Inky gets it, too," Mercy murmured. "I don't know if I'm doing it right, but it *feels* right."

Rowan chuckled, lifting her head up so she could see what wonders Ray was doing with her lean, fit, super flexible body. She was slowly, methodically, masterfully putting her hand to elbow parallel to the floor while her body bent back until her feet were over her head. It made Rowan feel sleepy.

"We're like, I don't know, twenty years younger than cousin Ray?" Rowan said. "Shouldn't we have youth on our side?"

"One would think."

A second goat came over to Rowan, sniffed her face, licked her nose, seemed to approve of her taste, then climbed up in between Petunia and her chin.

"Okay." Ray came out of her pose gracefully and then stood facing the class. "Please lie flat on your back, close your eyes and let all of your muscles relax."

"Hey!" Rowan told the goats. "One minute you're behind, and then the next minute you're ahead." And then she realized that the second goat was closing off her airway and she had to sit up.

Ray was sitting upright, legs tucked beneath her supple body, hands resting on her knees. She opened her eyes and looked at Rowan, smiled and gave her a thumbs-up. She could really put lipstick on a pig, turning anything seemingly negative into a positive.

After Ray guided all of the participants back into a seated position, hands together in a namaste gesture, she led them in chanting om. At the end, she said, "Peace," and all of the class attendees clapped for Ray and the goats.

Rowan felt lucky to experience it. Ray was booked for a month, but the triplets were giving her full family passes. She thought they would do it even if she turned out to be a cousin fifteen times removed. They were just that way.

"Mercy." Rowan shook her friend's arm.

Mercy stirred, snorted loudly, and then opened one eye, her face smooshed into the yoga mat. "What?"

"The class is over."

"It is?"

"Uh-huh."

"It went by so fast." Mercy started to get up slowly and gently so Inky could dismount. Then she pushed herself up and rolled over to her side.

Ray was still offering affirmations and encouragement as she said goodbye to the attendees. "Just remember, it's called yoga practice because it takes time and persistence."

Sitting upright, Mercy yawned while hugging Inky. "I need to practice eating a cheeseburger."

"Oh yeah," Rowan agreed. "I would give anything for a crinkle fry and some sweet barbecue sauce."

"Yummy."

The room had cleared, and Ray began to pick up the mats. Rowan and Mercy got back on their feet and helped. The goats, who knew their routine very well now, congregated at the door, waiting for Ray to take them back to the barn.

"Did you enjoy it?" Ray asked as they were wiping down the mats and sweeping up any droppings. Later the floor would be cleaned with a disinfectant safe for the environment and the sensitive little goats.

"I did," Rowan said. "My body doesn't want to bend

anywhere close to what you were doing. You're really impressive."

Ray ducked her head, shook it and waved her hand as if swatting away the compliment. "I like it. Kept me sane during the last decade of my marriage."

Rowan and Mercy laughed.

"Well, I shouldn't really say that," Ray added.

"If it's true, you sure as heck should," Rowan said. "It's your life and your experience."

Ray walked over and hugged her. "I'm so glad we found each other."

"Me, too," Rowan said.

"Me three," Mercy added.

They walked the goats back to the barn where they had delicious snacks of sunflower seeds and sliced apples. A little sweet treat that the goats knew awaited them after class.

"Now that we have more goats, we rotate them regularly so they have enough rest and just time to be a goat," Ray said, directing the goats to their specific bowls. "This entire barn will be for the goats. And they love muffins." She stopped to love on her miniature donkeys who were braying for their own snack. The donkeys couldn't partake in the muffins, so a couple of carrot slices went a long way without adding too much sugar to their diets.

"It's amazing what you've done," Rowan said.

"Thank you," Ray said as they walked out of the barn. Once outside, she pointed to a building in the distance on the other side of the pasture built for the miniature cows. "That is my next project. Make that barn a mini cow haven."

"Love that," Mercy said.

"Totally love that," Rowan agreed.

"I have this idea for a Cuddle Cows experience," Ray said, clasping her hands excitedly. "Those babies love to cuddle, love to be brushed, love to play ball. People can come from all over to cuddle these cows!"

"I want to cuddle those cows right now," Rowan said.

Ray smiled at her broadly. "Family discount."

As they approached the firepit, a brand-new Mercedes-Benz SUV pulled into the common area and parked. It had tinted windows and a shiny gold flake paint job that sparkled in the sunlight.

"Okay. That's cool."

"Danny enjoys an upgrade." Ray laughed. "I upgrade my cow's living quarters, and she upgrades her vehicles. Everyone is happy!"

Danny waved at them as she got out of her SUV, her blond bobbed hair framing her face beautifully. She walked around to the back of her vehicle, opened the hatchback, pulled down a ramp, and a rotund pig slowly made its way down the ramp.

"Do my eyes deceive me?" Mercy asked with a smile.

"Nope." Danny shook her head, her ponytail bouncing. "Your eyes are working just fine. That is Lu-Lu."

Danny walked over to them holding a gold, jewel-encrusted leash that not only matched her Mercedes but also Lu-Lu's leotard.

"Hi, all!" Danny said.

Everything about Danny screamed high-class boss woman with a flair for the dramatic.

"That's a nice ride, coz," Rowan said.

"Isn't it, darling?" Danny asked. "Now, I am going to tell you something that you may not believe, but I swear on my entire Birkin collection that Lu-Lu picked the color for me. Now, I see your skepticism. It wasn't a replicable randomized control trial or anything that serious. But I put my final three colors on the ground and let Lu-Lu get a good look at them. She put her pretty little cloven hoof on Kalahari Gold Magno three times in a row."

They all laughed good-naturedly, and so did Danny, looking down at her pig. "You are mama's smart baby girl, aren't you?" she crooned.

Danny looked out at the building in the distance. "Wayne is assessing the cow barn now. He'll make a list of materials and labor, and we'll set a budget. But." Danny lowered her Chanel sunglasses at Ray. "Do you really need a state-of-the-art barn for your cows? It's going to cost a pretty penny."

Ray lowered her own glasses. "Do you really need a new Mercedes?"

Danny pushed her glasses back up her nose. "Touché. Carry on." And with that, she turned on her heel and walked with her pig to the main house.

"Do you know what, Ray?" Rowan said. "You triplets are cool."

Ray laughed. "We think you're pretty darn cool, too."

* * *

Axel was with Wayne assessing a building for the next big project on the ranch. Wayne had climbed up a ladder to check the roof, looking for any wood planks that were salvageable. The building was in such bad shape from years of neglect, it had gone to seed. Weeds and brush pushed up from the ground in between the planks that had survived.

"It's the whole darn ball of wax." Wayne dragged his hand through his silver hair before he put his cowboy hat back on. "We'd be lucky to just salvage some boards and a couple of windows over there."

"Tin from the roof could be up-cycled one way or another. But it's long past its providing shelter days."

"Yeah, you called it," Wayne agreed, pulling off his work gloves and putting them in his back pocket. "This isn't going to work, no way, no how."

"What's Ray want to use it for?"

Wayne shook his head on the way out of the building. "She wants a custom, luxury facility for her cows."

Axel cocked his head, knowing he looked confused. "Come again?"

Wayne pointed at him. "Exactly."

"I've never heard of that before."

"Buddy, that is the whole truth," Wayne said, scratching his white goatee in thought. "But there's been a lot I've never heard of before I came here. The triplets are their own special blend. I'd like to marry Charlie one day, so I'm pretty much the silent partner in all of this mess." He crossed his arms in front of his body, sizing up the building and formulating some thoughts. "Ray wants hot water bath areas, big commercial dryers, grooming areas and sleeping quarters."

Axel just stood by while the older cowboy worked through his thoughts. It was probably best for him not to say that this whole venture seemed plum crazy. Maybe Ray was consuming edibles.

"I just can't wrap my head around it," Wayne finally concluded. "There's not a chance that this tinderbox is going to become usable space. It needs to be stripped for parts and demolished."

Axel couldn't disagree.

"Is that how you see it?" Wayne surprised him by asking.

He nodded.

"Yep," Wayne said with a sigh. "Let's go tell the bosses that this here is a no-go."

Together, they walked through the pasture where the mini cows were settling in nicely. Axel wasn't sure how he would feel about this kind of ranching; he wasn't an old timer, but he was a traditional rancher. Here in Big Sky, with the ski life attracting some of the wealthiest humans on earth to snap up the inventory and charge massive fees for a weekend trip, it had been difficult to find his way of life. If he hadn't run into Wayne on his way through Gallatin Gateway when he stopped to gas up his truck, he sure as heck wouldn't be in Big Sky, and he wouldn't have met Rowan.

Gosh darn, he couldn't believe that he'd almost missed out on a badass, major boss cowgirl like Rowan.

He'd been searching for something, someone, that would fit into the ideal of his future. He'd been town to town, looking for a woman like Rowan. A woman built for ranching. A woman built for tough times, lean times, but a love for the land that formed an unbreakable bond. Ranching was his life. Ranching was his past. Ranching had to be his future. And he supposed he figured that out just lately. He had been pulled to return to his life next to his family. But that was before Rowan. She was the kind of woman who could marry a rancher and settle down into that life with him. No neighborhood, no matter how appealing and familiar, could replace the life he had as a rancher. Rowan could be that missing piece to complete the picture of his forever.

"Well, looky here!" Cody Ty met them at the fence. "Who in the world is this? I thought you'd skipped town."

Axel smiled at him. Danny wanted him to have the time to build a romance with Rowan and had given him a whole lot of time on the clock, but not necessarily on the job. "I do as my boss tells me," he said.

Cody Ty grinned at him. "It's great work if you can find it." Then the old rodeo champ asked, "What's up with that building out yonder?"

Wayne shook his head. "Ray."

"Oh Lordy," Cody Ty said. "What in the world is that woman cookin' up now?"

"Cuddle Cows," Wayne told him. "Picture this. Hot water baths, blowouts, grooming and cuddling."

Cody Ty wasn't often speechless, but he appeared to have arrived. "You know what? I didn't know what the heck she was up to with those goats, but my lady love says it's a booming business. Who knows? Maybe she's the future, and we're just relics of the past. But I am going to tell you this right here and right now, as God is my witness, I am not going to cuddle none of those cows. I'm drawing the line."

Axel liked the company of men who had life experience and wisdom to pass on. And he'd already learned from them that if he found a good woman, he needed to put a ring on that finger. And he knew that he had found such a woman in Rowan.

As if he had thought of her and she appeared, Rowan was walking from the main house toward her cabin.

"Boys," Axel said, "I see my future walking over there. Watch and learn." He climbed to the top board of the fence, easily hopped over and started running toward Rowan.

He did hear Wayne say to Cody Ty, "Boys?"

Then Cody Ty said, "Watch and learn? Heck, those young bucks don't know their own backside from a baboon."

Well, Axel thought as he closed the space between himself and the prettiest redhead he'd ever seen, maybe they were right. Maybe he didn't know his own backside from a baboon. But he was a quick learner, and he did know one thing: he surely did love Rowan Brand.

Rowan had gone for a stroll to clear her head. She had had a very difficult conversation with her mom. Her mom wanted the best for her, she really did, and Rowan didn't doubt that, but encouraging Dutton to come to Montana to win her back was so out of line that Rowan had to, respectfully, let her mom know that it was over with Dutton. Case closed.

"It's been real hard here, Rowan," Marla had told her. "I know that I was wrong to send Dutton there. I do know that, and I am sorry. But I can't hardly go anywhere without someone pulling me aside and giving me heartfelt condolences as if you had died. I've taken to staying home, shutting my blinds."

"I'm sorry, Mama. I truly am." And Rowan meant it. Her parents had taken a huge financial hit, but money could be made and replenished. The real hit was more personal. The fabric that bound their community together was coming apart at the seams, and the elastic had been stretched to the point that it would never snap back into place.

The hardest part of the conversation was when her mother shed tears. Now she understood, from this experience, what it must be like to be a parent who couldn't stop their child from getting injured or feeling pain. She was helpless to ease her mother's pain.

"Mama. I remember a very smart woman once told me that this moment right here is going to pass, the drama is going to be yesterday's news. And you were right, Mama. Everything will go back to normal. A new normal. Until then, we will lean on each other."

"I love you, baby girl."

"I love you."

As she hung up the phone, Rowan knew that, sooner rather than later, she would have to tell her mother about Axel. She hadn't heard it yet, but the clock was ticking. When she started to venture out, started accepting invitations again, going to church and running into folks, her mother would absolutely find out. Rowan had to find the exact right time; she couldn't put it off for too much longer. She had to be the one to break it to Marla. Her dad would go with the flow; he didn't let himself get caught up with anything outside of his own bubble. Her brother would be thrilled she had moved on; he'd always thought Dutton was an idiot.

She was still very much inside of her own head when she heard her name and turned to see Axel running full tilt toward her. Before he reached her, she smiled and laughed. It immediately pulled her right out of her head into the present moment.

Axel reached her, picked her up in a bear hug and swung her around. When he put her down, she was dizzy in the best possible way. She was laughing and happy and so in love. Yes, in love. They had used the *L* word but never preceded by the very important, two-letter word *in*. But she knew it. She felt it.

Axel kissed her. Right there in the common area of the ranch, right in front of the windows in the main house where Danny had set up her business hub. It was a declaration that he had found love at Hideaway Ranch. It was a declaration that he would gladly put himself up on that wall of couples if she would stand beside him.

"Gosh darn it, babe." Axel looked down into her deep blue eyes. "I sure do fancy you."

Rowan tilted her head to the side, looking up at him with that sweetness and kindness that he had grown to depend on. "I sure do fancy you, cowboy."

He kissed her again, just for good measure. "It's not quittin' time just yet. But I sure would like to dance with you tonight. Under the stars. Would you like that?"

"Yes. I would."

He brought her hand to his lips and kissed it. "Then it's a date."

Nash had Mercy on the brain. That wasn't anything new. Even when he was with an incredible, brilliant, drop-dead gorgeous, sweet-as-cotton-candy woman like Magdalena, Mercy was his love. Unrequited. Until the day she kissed him.

That moment had been played over and over again in his mind, and he was concerned that he was attaching all sorts of deep meaning to that kiss that didn't exist. He was afraid that Mercy, in a spontaneous moment, was confused by her sudden broken engagement with Douglas. That was enough to make anyone off-kilter. But it had served to give him hope when there had never been hope before for nearly two decades. That was why he had kept to himself and focused on his books. He would let Mercy come to him, when and if she was ever ready.

It felt like a month, but it had only been a few days after the kiss. He was in his bunk, noise-canceling headphones on while he read, in an attempt to drown out the noise generated by an influx of new ranch hands. Men came and went. That was the name of the ranching game. Drifters, nomads, rolling stones. He was so focused on his book, he didn't hear his name being called. It was only when a wiry cowpoke with buck teeth and a buzz cut started banging his fist on his bunk that he even noticed someone was trying to get his attention.

Annoyed, he snatched his headphones off. "What the heck, dude?"

The cowpoke hitched his thumb over his shoulder. "You've got company."

Nash sat up and looked over at the door. There stood Mercy, her arms crossed in front of her body. The moment he saw her, his heart started to race. He had hoped she would come to him, but he had been ninety-nine percent sure he would be out of luck again.

He yanked off his headphones, swung out of his bunk and walked a straight line to her.

"Can we talk?" Mercy asked.

"Of course we can." He put his arm around her.

It was forecasted to rain. The clouds in the sky were blocking out the stars, but it was cool. A perfect night for a walk.

"Are you all right?" he asked her.

Her shoulders were slumped forward, her arms still crossed as if she had a chill in her bones. "I am," she replied quietly. "Can we go to your bench?"

Nash felt like she'd socked him in the gut. He actually stopped in his tracks. Mercy knew about his bench? "If that's what you want."

"It is."

Together they walked to the small path that would take him to the small clearing and his hideaway bench. There was some light filtering through the trees and brush that lit the path, and then they were there. He had dreamed of sitting with Mercy in this special spot he had found.

Could it really be that Danny's campaign that *love is always in season* at Hideaway Ranch wasn't a gimmick? Maybe there was magic here. If there was, could that magic finally allow Mercy to see that he was the man she had always dreamed of? Could this magic allow Mercy to see that they had always been meant to be?

Chapter Sixteen

Mercy didn't know if she deserved this moment with Nash. She wanted to deserve it. She did. He was beside her as he always was, strong, kind, loving. He took her hand in his, and she held on to it. The hardest part of what she had been mulling over was the fact that the first person she wanted to tell everything to was Nash. And when she lost that right after they arrived in Montana, she'd felt lonelier than she had at any other point in her life. Nash was home to her.

"I wanted to sit here with you," she said quietly.

"I had no idea that you knew about this bench."

"I did."

There was a pause, and he let her breathe, let her find her way to the words she wanted to say.

"I feel so embarrassed," Mercy said with an insecure laugh.

"No," Nash said. "You don't have to be embarrassed with me. I love you, Mercy. That has never changed, that will never change. Our paths may take us in completely different directions, but my heart will always belong with yours. No matter the miles between us."

Mercy dropped her head and put her free hand over

her mouth, trying to hold back her tears. Her sorrow. She needed to come clean. It had to be tonight, while she still had her nerve. The clouds overhead, blocking the stars, gave her a blanket of darkness that allowed her to hide, even as she planned on exposing herself in a way she had never done before.

"I know about this bench," Mercy said to Nash. "I saw you here. Sitting with Magdalena. You were laughing with her. And…" She had to pause. Why was this so hard to say? Why? "I felt so envious of her."

"Envious of her?"

She nodded, and the tears she had tried to hold back won the battle. She sniffed loudly, and that sent Nash digging in his front pocket for a handkerchief. When he handed it to her, the gesture made her laugh through her tears.

"You always have a handkerchief at the ready just in case I started to cry."

"My grandmother taught me that every gentleman should have a handkerchief, just in case."

"I really miss her."

"Me, too."

This bond that they shared, built on thousands of uneventful days, had turned into a solid foundation upon which so many of their shared memories were built. They had a common history, loved the same people and embraced the same values. That, Mercy realized, was love. Plain, simple, uncomplicated love.

"Nash." She said his name.

"Mercy."

"I didn't realize this until I ended things with Douglas." She breathed in deep and just blurted it out as fast as she could. "I love you."

"I know you do. I love you, too. We will always be friends, Mercy. No matter what. I promise. We will."

"Damn it, Nash! Quit being so damn agreeable and hear what I'm telling you." She turned her body toward him and took both of his hands in hers. "I did everything in my power to keep you beside me because I am in love with you."

Their eyes had adjusted to the dim light, and she could see plainly that he looked stunned. Without a word, he stood up, paced around and then stood before her, his hand rubbing the back of his neck. Then he sat down.

"Did you hear me, Nash?"

"Yeah. I did. Yes."

Now she had to stand up and pace. Of all the reactions she had imagined, this was not one of the options. She just told the man who had claimed to be in love with her for decades that *she* loved *him*, and he didn't embrace her, kiss her or tell her to get lost because he was now in love with Magdalena. After pacing in a circle, she sat back down next to Nash and just waited because now she really didn't know what else to do.

Finally, Nash asked, "Are you serious, Mercy? You're in love with me?"

"Yes." It was the unvarnished truth. Her truth, covered up by years of family expectations, community expectations and her own lack of self-worth that stopped her from breaking things off with Douglas years ago.

"How? When?"

She took his hands in hers. "I don't know. I don't. I just know that when Douglas was out of the way, my feelings, my true feelings long denied, bubbled up."

In the silence, Mercy wondered if this was all too little too late. She was about to get up, to run back to the cabin and pack up her things, and then she was in Nash's strong arms, his lips on hers, her body pulled close, and it was magic.

Magic. The feel of her body connecting with his was fire. There in the dark, with the man she had shared every bit of herself with, except her heart, she found passion. Heat. Lust.

"I love you, Mercy." Nash held her close, so close she could feel the rapid beating of her heart. It matched the rhythm of her own.

The smell of his skin, the feel of his hands on her body, it was all electric. How had she gone so many years without knowing this existed?

"How can this be?" Nash asked. "Are you really mine?"

Mercy took his face in her hands. "If you want me, I am yours."

"I can't remember a time when I didn't want you as my own, Mercy. And I will want you for the rest of my days. As long as I take a breath, I will want you. I will love you."

"Then, I am yours."

"Where are you taking me?" Rowan asked, feeling free for the first time in so many years. She felt free to goof off, free to laugh and free to love someone new. Someone amazing, like Axel Redford.

"Skinny-dipping." Axel had his truck in four-wheel drive as it took the bumps and divots in one of the less used back roads that allowed access to different parts of the ranch.

"How do you read my mind?" she asked. The minute she first saw that lake, she had wanted to peel off her clothes and jump in.

"I have planned your perfect date."

"Oh, you have?"

"Yes, beautiful. I really have."

"Tell me."

"First, Cassady's famous sangria and a cheese and cracker charcuterie board from Ray."

"Did you just use the word *charcuterie*?"

"I'm classy, babe."

"I'm not. Can you define a charcuterie board for me?"

"Sure. It's a wooden doodad with cheese and stuff on it."

"Thank you." She laughed out loud. "Perfect description."

"I told you. Hang with me, and I'm gonna class you right up."

The truck hit a big pothole, and the suspension of the truck jostled her and set her off laughing again. She felt like a giddy teenager with Axel. They hadn't talked much about their future, but she knew that if their love grew into something more permanent, they would always laugh together, making tough times just a bit easier to navigate.

They reached the lake, and Axel set up the sangria and the finger foods on the tailgate of his truck, kept the truck running so they had some light, and the diesel burned slowly. He found a playlist of romantic country songs. Then Axel easily picked her up so she could sit on the tailgate next to the finger food.

"This is actually a charcuterie board," Rowan said, popping a grape into her mouth. "How am I going to survive without Cassady and Ray? I will starve."

"It'll be a real shame to lose you like that."

She punched him on the arm playfully and was given a kiss for her effort. She sipped on the sangria and felt happy. What a strange and wonderful feeling. How was it possible she had never felt it before with Dutton? She had been sleepwalking, one predetermined step after predetermined step. Rinse and repeat.

Axel had his fill of the sangria and snacks and then he offered his hand to her. "May I have this dance?"

"Absolutely."

He lifted her up and let her down slowly. Then he took her in his arms, and they began to dance. As he dipped her, she could feel raindrops on her face.

"It's raining," she said, her head tilted back, her hair swinging as he brought her back into his arms.

"Do you care?"

"Wyoming cowgirls don't melt!"

"Thank God for Wyoming cowgirls."

They danced until they were out of breath, and then they stripped off their clothes and picked through the grass hand in hand until they reached the bank of the lake. Rowan slipped her hand out of his and ran into the water, splashing up water as she went until she turned around to face him.

"Are you coming, rancher?"

Axel dove in and surfaced in front of her. She swam into his arms and wrapped her legs around his waist, and they kissed as the raindrops caused the lake water to dance all around them. It was a moment so beautiful in its simplicity. A glass of sangria, a charcuterie board, dancing to romantic country classics and now skinny-dipping in the rain, kissing her handsome cowboy. Would life ever be this perfect again?

When the water turned cold, Axel ran back to the truck, grabbed towels and then ran back to her so he could wrap her up in the towel. Laughing, they made it into the back seat, heater turned on, and they huddled together, drawing warmth from each other. And then there were more kisses to share.

"I managed to get the sangria," Axel said once they had dried off and managed to get most of their clothes back on. "I think I'm going to have to buy Ray a new charcuterie board."

With a full glass of sangria, Rowan said, "This is one of the best nights of my life."

Axel leaned back so he could look at her. "God, you are a beautiful woman, Rowan."

"I feel beautiful when I'm with you."

"You should feel beautiful all of the time, whether you're with me or not."

"I'll work on it."

"See that you do," he said with a wink. Then he added, "I've got something I need to tell you."

"Oh crap. You're married."

"No."

"Wanted by the law?"

"Will you let me say my piece?"

"Sorry."

"I need to tell you something," he repeated. "This is important."

"Okay."

"I love you. You know that already," he said. "But it's more serious than that for me. I'm in love with you, Row."

She put her hand on his face. "I feel like I'm in love with you."

"Is that right?"

"Yes, it is," she said and then asked teasingly, "But was this truly the place to profess said love?"

"Woman." Axel took the glass of sangria out of her hand, drank what remained, and then he wrapped her up in his arms. "How do you feel about necking in the back of my truck?"

"I'm for it."

"Rowan Reese Brand, where have you been all my life?"

"I know this is hard on all of you, but it's time for me to leave," Cassady said at breakfast the next morning.

"It's flown by," Rowan said. "I don't feel like I'm the same person who drove onto this ranch."

"Neither do I," Mercy said.

"Hideaway Ranch has helped us grow," Cassady said. "I think we should come back once a year. No matter where we live, what we're doing, we return."

Rowan and Mercy agreed. Nash arrived to help Cassady with their baggage. Once he had it loaded into their rental, Cassady turned back to them with watery eyes. The three of them hugged, but Nash held back.

"Come here and hug me this instant, Nash Landry," Cassady said.

Nash chuckled and joined the group hug.

Rowan and Mercy watched Cassady and Nash get into the car. Then Rowan called out to Cassady, "Text us when you touch down in NYC."

Cassady rolled down the window. "I'm going to Wyoming first. Say hi to the fam."

Together, they waved to Cassady until they disappeared around the bend.

"Does that seem like a good idea to you?" Mercy asked her as they headed back inside.

"Nope," Rowan said.

"That's my gut response," Mercy agreed. "Everyone is still adjusting to not just one but two major breakups. Between you and me, we have six degrees of separation. Our lives touch everyone in some sort of way."

"Then sprinkle some Cassady on top? There's going to be some sort of meltdown."

Rowan nodded. "Yep. It's just a matter of time."

Once inside of their cabin, they each grabbed a cup of coffee and landed in the sitting room with its floor-to-ceiling picture windows. During the day, they showed off the striking landscape, and at night, it was the perfect place to look for shooting stars.

They settled into the oversize and overstuffed couch cushions, and Rowan realized that this might be the moment they finally discussed the evening that Douglas and Dutton showed up at the ranch. Perhaps from the outside looking in, it might seem strange to bury this conversation to be dug up later, but Mercy and she shared a mutual flaw—if they didn't talk about it, they could pretend that it didn't exist.

"Have you spoken with Doug?" Rowan asked, jump-starting the conversation.

"No." Mercy put her coffee cup on the side table. "One day I will. When I'm in the grocery store or in a restaurant. Until then, I am focusing on the future."

"Same," she said. "Everyone involved needs a cooling-off period."

Mercy laughed. "I think I need a cooling-off decade."

"Even better." Rowan laughed along with her dear friend.

After they quieted, Mercy said, "I do have news."

Rowan waited and listened.

"Nash and I are together."

Rowan sat up straighter. "Together, together?"

Mercy nodded, a small self-conscious smile on her heart-shaped face. "We love each other."

"Mercy." Rowan felt choked up with happiness for her dear friends. She scooted over to where Mercy was sitting and hugged her. "I am so happy for you. The both of you."

"Thank you. I feel at peace," Mercy said. "And what about you and the handsome Mr. Redford?"

"It's love," Rowan admitted. "But nothing like I've experienced before."

"Hideaway has worked its magic on both of us, it seems."

Rowan laughed, wiping away some happy tears. "You know we're going to end up on Danny's wall of fame."

"Of course we will," Mercy agreed. "It was simply meant to be."

"There really is some sort of magic here," Rowan said thoughtfully. "We both fell in love."

"And Cassady fell in love with herself."

Later that evening, Rowan was restless in bed. She threw off the bedsheet and got up to scrounge around the kitchen. Cassady's cooking was sorely missed. She opened her door that led to the mutual landing with Mercy's room, and as it always seemed to happen, they were doing the same thing at the same time.

Mercy was wearing a large shirt that came down to her bare thighs. She was barefoot, and her hair was mussed.

"Is that Nash's shirt?"

"Yes." Mercy met her at the top step. "What's the matter with that?"

Rowan covered her eyes. "I don't know. I just wasn't mentally prepared for it. It's so weird."

"You're being weird." Mercy headed downstairs.

"Now I have a mental picture," Rowan complained.

"It's like the time I discovered that my parents actually had to have sex in order to conceive me."

"Rowan! Now I have a picture of your mom and dad." Mercy lowered her voice to a loud whisper. *"Naked."*

"Oh. Sorry. My bad."

They went into the kitchen, turned on the light, both of them blinking as their eyes adjusted. Mercy opened the fridge and began to fish around for some snacks that she could take upstairs while Rowan sat down at the table with a bowl of cereal. After Mercy gathered up chips and dip and two sodas, she stopped by the table and said, "Nash and I are moving to California together."

Rowan had been focused on her cereal but stopped chewing and looked at her childhood friend.

"I know it's unexpected, but I have to follow my heart," Mercy said. "And my heart is with Nash."

Rowan chewed quickly, swallowed, and then stood up to hug her friend. "I'm happy for you."

"Thank you," Mercy said. "I'm going back to school. I have my bachelor's in counseling, so I'm going to be applying to the UC Berkeley master's counseling program."

Rowan was able to give Mercy another hug when her phone started ringing. "It's past midnight. That can't be good news." She picked up her phone. It was her mom.

"Mama, are you okay? Is Dad okay?"

"Yes, sweetheart, we are. It's your brother."

"What did he do now?"

"Well." Her mother sighed. "He got in a fight with Dutton. Broke his nose, Lord help us."

Rowan put the phone on speaker so Mercy could hear.

"Why would he do that!"

"Dutton was saying something about some rancher at that ranch you're staying at."

She exchanged a look with Mercy. She had waited too late.

"Said something bad enough for your brother to sock it to him. You know Habit."

They called her brother Habit because he had a habit of finding trouble. "Yep. I sure do."

"Dad's down at the police station bailing him out. He's gonna bail Cassady while he's at it."

"They're in jail?" Mercy exclaimed. "What did *they* do?"

"Lord give me strength, Cassady punched Douglas in the nose. Broke for sure."

"Oh. No." Mercy dropped her head into her hands.

They wanted to be done with their relationships with Douglas and Dutton, but bodily harm never factored into that decision.

"What a mess," Mercy said.

"I just don't know what Dutton was going on about. If you *had* met someone, you would have told me."

"Mama. I do need to tell you something. I don't think it would've made a difference because Habit does what he does. But maybe if I would have, Habit wouldn't have done this, and that makes me feel horrible. No one can know if one thing or another would change the outcome. Every single variable has a cause and effect."

"Rowan Reese," her mother interrupted. "What are you trying to tell me so unsuccessfully?"

"I *did* meet somebody."

Her mother went silent.

"I was going to tell you, Mama, I just wanted things to settle a bit on your end."

"Is this someone worth mentioning?"

Rowan bit her lip. How could her mother make her feel like a kid who had been caught necking with a neighborhood boy? "He is, yes, ma'am." She just had to go on and get through to the other side. "His name is Axel, and he's a rancher by way of Colorado."

Another lengthy pause, and when Nash opened the door, shirtless, Mercy hurried over to him and they both went back up to her room.

"So, Dutton was telling the truth, and now your brother is in jail? Dutton is going to press charges, no two ways about it."

"Mama. I have no idea what Dutton said to Habit, but I sure as heck don't believe it had more than a kernel of truth. He's always egged Habit on, and now that our engagement isn't a shield, Habit socked him but good. It doesn't make much difference to the law, but I'd bet dollars to donuts that he deserved it. And that goes for Douglas, too."

"Well." Her mother sighed heavily. "You may as

well tell me about this man you met. You say he's a rancher?"

"Yes, ma'am, he surely is." Rowan had a smile in her voice. "A rancher to his core."

Chapter Seventeen

The next night, she was lying in the bed of Axel's truck on her back, gazing up at the stars, her head resting on his shoulder. "It seems strange to be leaving tomorrow."

"It's exciting," Axel said. "I've had itchy feet for a while now."

Rowan thought about that for a minute and then asked, "Are you ever going to be ready to settle down? I mean, right now, all you have is a duffel bag and a truck."

He looked over at her. "Are you wanting a promise here?"

"I guess."

"I'm devoted to you, babe. Whatever you want, I'll do my damnedest to get it for you," he said. "Are you looking for marriage? If you are, I'm ready. We can stop on the way out of town and get hitched."

"No," she told him. "I'm not ready to be engaged or think of getting married right now. I want to be settled, married and pregnant by the time I'm thirty."

Axel shifted his body toward her, kissed her and

said, "Rowan, when you're ready, we are going to make the most beautiful babies."

She laughed. "You're so sure of me."

"Well, of course I am," he said. "I wouldn't be here if I wasn't."

For a while they shared a comfortable silence, gazing up at the stars in the expansive blue-black sky.

"You've never asked me about my past with Dutton. Heck, you didn't even ask me questions about the day he showed up."

"I've seen the highlight reel. The guy's a tool."

She laughed. "Tell me how you really feel about him." She curled her body into his, loving the feeling of his lean, muscular body next to hers. She put her hand on his heart. "You've never told me about your past. How come?"

She felt his body tense, his jaw tighten. "I don't like to look back. I'm not going that way."

"But you've been hurt. You told me one day you'd tell me about it."

He gave the smallest lift of the shoulder. "Haven't we all been hurt? What's the point of dredging it up all the time?"

She pushed herself up so she could really look into his face. "Tell me, Axel. There are times in a relationship where you have to open up the banged-up parts of your heart. That's called intimacy."

Axel reached up to pull her into his body. "If it's intimacy you want, come on and get it, beautiful."

"Not that kind of intimacy, Axel! Emotional intimacy!" She sat up entirely and crossed her arms in front of her body.

"You're really getting ticked off over this, babe. Why?"

"Because I let you know me." She pointed to her chest. "I let you in. You've seen the best of me, and you've heard about the worst of me. It's not comfortable, there are so many things I wish I could go back and change, but I can't. You share *nothing* with me. A relationship can't survive that way."

Axel sat up now. He seemed to be figuring out that she wasn't just going to let it ride.

"I need more. If I'm going to meet your family, travel around the country, see the sights and build a foundation with you, you have to let me in. Otherwise, I'll just go home."

"Wait a minute," Axel said, his tone frustrated. "I brought you out here for some romance under the stars and now you want to fight?"

"I'm serious."

"I can darn well see that." He raked his fingers through his hair, pushing it back from his forehead. "What do you want to know?"

She turned her head back in his direction. "Who *was* she?"

"Damn." He had his arms resting on his bent knees, shaking his head. "Can't seem to outrun this shadow."

She listened. This was the time for him to either put his chips on the table or go cash his chips in.

"Who was she? High school sweetheart. Then, fiancée. And then, my ex."

"Sounds neat and tidy. Not like most breakups I know."

"It was not neat and tidy, that's for dang sure," Axel said in a serious tone. "For a while there, I worked on an oil rig. Damn good money. We were saving for a house."

"That's serious."

"Sure was. I sure was," Axel said. "I came home early. A surprise."

"Oh."

"Do I need to tell you the rest?"

"No." She put her hand on his arm. "I got the picture."

"Well, not the whole picture. One missing piece to that puzzle. My best friend. Real tight from grade school right on up."

Her stomach twisted. "You lost two people all at once."

"The way I see it now? They did me a favor. They deserved each other. They got married. The last time I saw them was at a car show, and there they were. Overweight, missing teeth, and I thought, Lord, I dodged a bullet. His loss was my gain."

She let the story sink in, and then she rested her chin on his shoulder. "Thank you for sharing that with me."

"Are you done trying to fight with me?" he asked angrily.

"Sure," she said. "Do you want to kiss and make up?"

"Yeah. I think I do," he said. "Do you?"

"Yes, I do."

"Then come over here and kiss me, Spitfire!"

She obliged, sliding over and kissing him sweetly.

"That's quite a nickname you have for me, rancher."

"It's fitting."

"I suppose." She laughed.

"Can we drop this now?" Axel asked. "Or do you want to start another fight with me?"

"Yes, my love, we can drop it for good."

"All packed up." Rowan zipped her suitcase and then sat down next to it on the bed. This room had become a safe space, a cozy nest and a perfect nook for watching the rain or the birds flitting around in the nearby trees. She would miss it.

"Knock, knock." Mercy was at her door.

"Are you packed?"

Her friend nodded, walked over and sat down next to her.

"I'm not ready to leave," Rowan told Mercy. "This ranch has become a security blanket. I don't even know how Axel and I will be off this ranch, out in the real world."

"I am, but I'm not. I couldn't even imagine what changes I would experience here," Mercy said. "And I guess I'm ready to move on. See what else the universe has in store for me."

They leaned on each other, something they had always done. Their deep and abiding friendship seemed uncertain at the beginning of the trip. Now, it was as strong as tungsten steel.

The front door opened, and Nash called out to them.

"We're up here!" Mercy yelled down.

"Coming right up."

Nash appeared in the doorway, and he seemed, like Mercy, ready to get back home and figure out a new normal. Such a tight-knit community, with so many thick roots tangled together beneath the surface, would be difficult to navigate.

Mercy stood up and met Nash halfway. She stepped into his arms, hugged him tightly, and then they shared a sweet kiss. It was still odd to see them together romantically, but Rowan was so happy that they had found each other. Interesting that they had to find each other when they were right there together, all of the time.

"I'll grab that for you," Nash said, nodding to her suitcase.

"Naw. Thanks, though." Rowan waved him off. "I'm going to put my woman muscles to work."

He gave her a thumbs-up. "Let's see what you have, Mercy."

Mercy laughed and hooked her arm to his. "I have a whole lot of luggage, and I will not be using my woman muscles." She looked over her shoulder and winked at Rowan. "But I *will* be carrying my own purse."

While Nash worked on the chore of getting all of Mercy's luggage out into the rental, Mercy came out of the bedroom with an odd expression on her face.

"What's wrong?"

"I just found this in my jewelry box."

Mercy had a prized jewelry box from her grandmother, who had bought it with her first paycheck as a teacher. It was cream with a handle and five drawers of tufted leather and tiny gold balls.

Mercy held out her hand for Rowan to see. And for a second or two, it was difficult for her to make any rhyme or reason out of it.

In Mercy's palm was a heavy gold charm shaped into a boxing glove on a ball-and-bead chain. Cassady never took it off. It was their signature piece. They had been given it after their older brother had died of a rare throat cancer. Their brother had been an amateur boxer, and he had taught them how to fight in and out of the ring.

"That's Cassady's," Rowan said. "They never take that off."

Mercy teared up unexpectedly. "They left it where they knew I would find it. I always check and recheck my pieces in my jewelry box."

"I am shocked," Rowan said. It touched her that she was brought to tears. "What does the note say?"

Mercy opened the small card and inside was written in Cassady's loopy, frilly handwriting: "Mercy. The pupil has become the master. Love, C."

Mercy put her hand over her mouth, holding the glove in her other hand, her fingers closed tightly.

"Oh, come here." Rowan hugged her friend.

"I always thought that they hated me," Mercy said. "My sparkly everything, my makeup obsession, my healthy skin tips and tricks."

"They have wanted you to stand up for yourself, Mercy. They knew if you could stand up to them, you could stand up to anyone. Even Douglas."

Mercy nodded. "I did learn how to stand up for myself."

"That's why Cassady gave you this. Well." Rowan took the necklace. "Let's get this on you."

She put the necklace over Mercy's head and then moved her hair out of the way to clasp it.

Rowan turned her around. "It's perfect."

Mercy nodded, her fingers touching the boxing glove.

"Cassady loves you, I think we can agree on that now."

"Yes. We can," Mercy agreed. "And now, I actually think that I might love them, too. This ranch has all sorts of magic. Not just for lovers but for friends, too."

Axel arrived just as Nash was finishing packing Mercy up. "Man." Axel held out his hand to Nash. "I'm glad I met you."

"Same." Nash shook Axel's hand. "I'll see you in Wyoming. Right after Colorado?"

"Actually, we're flipping that deal. We'll be heading to Wyoming first. Her brother and Cassady."

"So I'll see you soon," Nash said. "I'll take you on a hunt for bones. Fair warning. It's addicting. Are you ready?" he asked Mercy.

"I am." She nodded, still touching the charm Cassady had bestowed upon her. "We'll stop at the main house and then hit the road."

They had decided to drive back to Wyoming, taking some time for themselves. The four of them went to the main cabin, and on the way, they ran into Charlie, who was holding a relaxed puppy in her arms.

"The cutest!" Rowan said.

"This is Jagger." Charlie smiled. "We have our big bruiser Bowie and we lost Wayne's dear Mick a while back. So Jagger just seemed to fit."

While they were fawning over the puppy, they could hear loud, ear-wrenching squeals coming from inside the main house.

"That's Lu-Lu," Charlie said, resigned. "She thinks Jagger is her baby. She cleans him, watches over him. And she gets very upset when he is out of her sight. She's taken to sleeping with him, but I'm worried she's going to squash him. Not on purpose, but she's robust."

The four of them followed Charlie into the ranch hub. Once Lu-Lu had Jagger back with her, she stopped with the awful squeals.

"There they are!" Danny was very happy to see them. Earlier in the morning, a photographer had stopped by to take their pictures for Danny's Couples Who Fell in Love wall.

"She finally got you on that wall," Charlie said. "I've got to get back to work, but don't be strangers."

"We won't." Rowan hugged her. "Thank you for embracing me, us, like we're super close kin."

Charlie looked at her with the same eyes that stared back at her reflection every morning, a deep sapphire blue. "Aren't we, though?"

"I suppose we are."

With that, Charlie headed out. Ray was cutting onions and crying. "It's just the onions," Ray said.

"It's the onions," Danny said. "But she's crying, too."

"I just hate it when people I love leave."

"Promise you will be back," Danny said.

"We will be back." Rowan hugged Ray. "I promise I'm not going to miss out on Cuddle Cows."

Ray hugged her and the rest of their crew. Then she kept right on cutting onions and crying.

"What do you think?" Danny said of their pictures on the wall.

"We love it," Rowan said.

Nash and Mercy, arm in arm, agreed.

"This land is magical," Danny said, not typically philosophical. "At first it was just a branding tool to bring as many bodies onto the ranch as I could. Bottom line first, everything else second. But I've changed."

"You really have," Ray agreed.

"That doesn't mean I'm going soft."

"No. Of course not," Rowan said.

"But the numbers don't lie," Danny went on. "Love is truly always in season at Hideaway Ranch."

They said their goodbyes with more promises to return. At the rental car, Nash and Axel hugged it out and made a deal to keep in touch along the way. Rowan and Mercy hugged for an extra long time, prompting Nash and Axel to remind them that they would be seeing each other in a week. Nash and Mercy had originally planned to take detours along the way to add to their list of zip-lining. But the legal trouble Cassady and Habit were embroiled in had made them change their plans.

It would be the shortest way back. And the same for Axel and Rowan. They would go to Colorado after Wyoming, and they wouldn't be meandering along on backcountry roads. That would have to be put on the back burner. Habit and Cassady needed them and that went to the top of the list for both of them. Axel had his arm around Rowan as they watched Nash back out, and they had a final wave until they drove out of sight.

"Well, I guess we're next."

"There's just one more thing I really want to do," Rowan said. "Okay?"

"Okay."

Axel was anxious to get on the road, but Rowan wasn't one to be rushed. She had it in her mind to visit the famous love tree where Butch Brand, the triplets' dearly departed father, had proposed to Rose Brand. When Rose agreed to marry him, Butch had carved their initials in an old gnarled tree, with twisted limbs but a massive trunk and heavy branches that stood the test of time.

"Ah," Rowan said, putting her hand over the initials carved in the tree. "Butch and Rose. Oh and look, these are Charlie's and Wayne's, Ray's and Dean's, and Danny's and Matteo's. It's so romantic. And look, that must be Cody Ty and his fiancée."

"I came to do the deed." Axel pulled out a large knife with a sharp blade, perfect for carving their initials with all the other Brand women. "Where do you want it?"

Rowan scouted the tree and finally found the perfect spot. "Here."

"Okay." Axel stepped up. "Watch and learn."

"Okay, cocky." She smiled at him, taking a seat on a nearby boulder with a flat spot perfect for her to sit and watch her man slay this dragon.

"It's fighting with me," Axel said. "But I'm going to win this battle."

As it turned out, carving into a tree with one hundred years of bark wasn't as easy as he'd first thought. Axel had to take several breaks, guzzling water. But what Rowan loved the most was the fact that her rancher did not give up. He fought his way through, going at it, then stepping back and figuring out another angle. After nearly an hour of work, Axel beckoned her over.

"Come here, babe."

She came up beside him, not at all off put by his sweat-drenched shirt. It was actually rather sexy.

"It's perfect," she said, hugging him. "Thank you."

He kissed the top of her head. "Anything for you."

And then her phone rang. A video call from Axel's sisters.

"Hey!" His sisters were both so happy when they saw her. It was unbelievable. They had embraced her completely, accepting her in a way she had never felt anywhere else beyond her own close-knit family.

"Are you guys heading out soon?" Joshua asked.

"We are," Rowan said. "Look what your brother did for me." She spun the phone around and showed Jane and Joshua the freshly carved letters.

"Oh!" Jane said. "That's so sweet, baby brother."

"Do you think it's weird that you guys call Rowan more than you call me?"

"No," Joshua and Jane said and looked at their brother as if he had just asked them something crazy.

"FYI, Axel. We are keeping her. So you'd better just make it work."

"Okay! Time to go!" Axel waved at his sisters.

"We love you, Row. And you, too, Axel."

"Gee, thanks," he said, but with a wink that meant he was taking the ribbing in good fun. "But we really have to go. We've got to head out."

"So responsible!" Joshua said. "Keep in touch."

As they hiked down the softly sloping hill that would lead them back to the central area of the ranch, Rowan had a sense of calm happiness that had never been in her repertoire of feelings. Axel didn't complete her; that was her job. But he filled her days with fun and adventure, he made her laugh, he was so damn handsome but a goofball behind closed doors.

And he showed her that he would choose her every single day. He wasn't afraid to love her openly, full throttle, win, lose or draw. He was fearless in love.

They reached his truck, and she felt so many emotions rising to the surface. "I will miss this place."

"It's not forever," Axel reassured her. "We'll be back."

He opened the door for her, and she climbed into the cab. Ray and Danny must have seen them through the window; they came out on the porch to wave goodbye.

Rowan waved out of the window until the main house disappeared from her view.

"You okay?"

She nodded. It was still a lot to process, the ending of her engagement in a moment of sheer humiliation in front of God and nearly the whole entire town, to running to Hideaway Ranch, quite literally to hide away. And now, here she was, with a new love, a new adventure and a future that wasn't planned out for her.

That had always scared her, but Axel had shown her the excitement of loosening her grip on the timeline and just letting the wind blow her in some direction. It could be the best time of her life.

"You're awfully quiet over there. Should I be worried?"

"No," she said. "I've been thinking about my channel. I want to get back to doing what I love, and I'm still a total romantic, so a love theme is a must. But I don't want to focus on the wedding. Now, I want to focus on love."

"I support you. One hundred percent."

"Thank you."

"Of course," he said.

As they pulled up to the gate leading off Hideaway Ranch property, she asked him, "Any regrets on your end?"

"Just one," Axel said.

"What is that?" Rowan asked, actually feeling a sinking feeling in her stomach.

He took her hand and kissed it. "My only regret is

that I didn't meet you earlier so I could love you longer."

"I can't believe I actually found a romantic rancher." She leaned over to give him one last kiss on Hideaway Ranch.

"Are you ready for the adventure of your life, babe?"

"I've been ready." She laughed. "Why are we still idling? Put the pedal to the metal."

"Darlin'." Axel shifted into gear and put his foot on the gas pedal. "Your wish is my command."

* * * * *

Get up to 4 Free Books!

We'll send you 2 free books from each series you try
PLUS a free Mystery Gift.

Both the **Harlequin® Special Edition** and **Harlequin® Heartwarming™** series feature compelling novels filled with stories of love and strength where the bonds of friendship, family and community unite.

YES! Please send me 2 FREE novels from the Harlequin Special Edition or Harlequin Heartwarming series and my FREE Gift (gift is worth about $10 retail). I may cancel anytime by emailing ReaderServiceInfo@Harlequin.com or by calling 1-800-873-8635.If I don't cancel, I will receive 6 brand-new Harlequin Special Edition books every month and be billed just $6.39 each in the U.S. or $7.19 each in Canada, or 4 brand-new Harlequin Heartwarming Larger-Print books every month and be billed just $7.19 each in the U.S. or $7.99 each in Canada, a savings of 20% off the cover price. It's quite a bargain! Shipping and handling is just 75¢ per book in the U.S. and $1.75 per book in Canada.* I understand that accepting the free books and gift places me under no obligation to buy anything—they are mine to keep for free no matter what I decide.

Choose one: ☐ **Harlequin Special Edition** (235/335 BPA G3CD) ☐ **Harlequin Heartwarming Larger-Print** (161/361 BPA G3CD) ☐ **Or Try Both!** (235/335 & 161/361 BPA G3CE)

Name (please print)

Address Apt. #

City State/Province Zip/Postal Code

Email: Please check this box ☐ if you would like to receive newsletters and promotional emails from Harlequin Enterprises ULC and its affiliates. You can unsubscribe anytime.

Mail to the **Harlequin Reader Service:**
IN U.S.A.: P.O. Box 1341, Buffalo, NY 14240-8531
IN CANADA: P.O. Box 603, Fort Erie, Ontario L2A 5X3

Want to explore our other series or interested in ebooks? Visit www.ReaderService.com or call 1-800-873-8635.

*Terms and prices subject to change without notice. Prices do not include sales taxes, which will be charged (if applicable) based on your state or country of residence. Canadian residents will be charged applicable taxes. Offer not valid in Quebec. This offer is limited to one order per household. Books received may not be as shown. Not valid for current subscribers to the Harlequin Special Edition or Harlequin Heartwarming series. All orders subject to approval. Credit or debit balances in a customer's account(s) may be offset by any other outstanding balance owed by or to the customer. Please allow 4 to 6 weeks for delivery. Offer available while quantities last.

Your Privacy — Your information is being collected by Harlequin Enterprises ULC, operating as Harlequin Reader Service. For a complete summary of the information we collect, how we use this information and to whom it is disclosed, please visit our privacy notice located at https://corporate.harlequin.com/privacy-notice. Notice to California Residents—Under California law, you have specific rights to control and access your data. For more information on these rights and how to exercise them, visit https://corporate.harlequin.com/california-privacy. For additional information for residents of other U.S. states that provide their residents with certain rights with respect to personal data, visit https://corporate.harlequin.com/other-state-residents-privacy-rights.

HSEHW2603